(K D

Miss Read, or in real life Dora Saint, was a school teacher by profession who started writing after the Second World War, beginning with light essays written for *Punch* and other journals. She then wrote on educational and country matters and worked as a scriptwriter for the BBC. Miss Read was married to a schoolmaster for sixty-four years until his death in 2004, and they have one daughter.

In the 1998 New Year Honours list Miss Read was awarded an MBE for her services to literature. She is the author of many immensely popular books, including two autobiographical works, but it is her novels of English rural life for which she is best known. The first of these, *Village School*, was published in 1955, and Miss Read continued to write about the fictitious villages of Fairacre and Thrush Green until her retirement in 1996. She lives in Berkshire.

D0274040

Books by Miss Read

Tyler's Row

* * *

Miss Read

Illustrated by J. S. Goodall

An Orion paperback
First published in Great Britain in 1972
by Michael Joseph Ltd
This paperback edition published in 2007
by Orion Books Ltd
Orion House, 5 Upper St Martin's Lane,
London WC2H 9EA

3 5 7 9 10 8 6 4

Copyright © Miss Read, 1972

The right of Miss Read to be identified as the
author of this work has been asserted by her in accordance
with the Copyright, Designs and Patents Act of 1988.

All rights reserved. No part of this publication may be
reproduced, stored in a retrieval system or transmitted,
in any form or by any means, electronic, mechanical,
photocopying, recording, or otherwise, without the prior
permission of the copyright owner.

A CIP catalogue record for this book
is available from the British Library.

ISBN 978 0 7528 8232 1

Typeset at The Spartan Press Ltd,
Lymington, Hants
Printed in Great Britain by Clays Ltd, St Ives plc

The Orion Publishing Group's policy is to use papers that
are natural, renewable and recyclable products and
made from wood grown in sustainable forests. The logging
and manufacturing processes are expected to conform to
the environmental regulations of the country of origin.

www.orionbooks.co.uk

For Helen
with love

CONTENTS

* * *

PART ONE

Outlook Unsettled

PART TWO

Some Squally Showers

PART THREE

Settled, With Some Sunshine

PART ONE

Outlook Unsettled

* * * *

1. Up for Sale

Nobody knows who Tyler was.

In fact, the general feeling in Fairacre is that there never was a Tyler, male or female.

'I can assure you, Miss Read,' the vicar, Gerald Partridge, told me one day when I inquired about the subject, 'that there is *not one* Tyler in the parish register! It's my belief that someone called *Taylor* built the four cottages. Taylor, as you know from your own school register, is a very common name in these parts.'

He rubbed his chin reflectively, a little concerned, I could see, about further explanation. The vicar, a living saint, dislikes hurting people's feelings, but is transparently truthful.

' "Taylor" can be so easily debased to "Tyler" if the diction is at all impure. It must have occurred many years ago, before schooling was so er – um . . .'

'Widespread?'

'Exactly. I doubt if it could happen now.'

I was not in agreement with the vicar on this last point, but forbore to say so. I am constantly correcting 'pile' for 'pail', 'tile' for 'tale'; arguing about 'pines of glass', 'rine-drops', and people arriving 'lite' for school. The vicar, though, would be most distressed at the thought of casting aspersions on my teaching, or the purity of the vowels of my pupils.

'I'm sure you're right about it once being "Taylor's Row",' I agreed. 'But it's too late to change it now.' We parted amicably.

*

Although mystery surrounds Tyler of Tyler's Row, yet the date of the building is in no doubt, for on the end cottage of the four is a carved stone bearing the inscription:

1763 AD

in beautiful curlicues, now much weathered by the sunshine and storms of two centuries, but still decipherable.

The row of four cottages stands at right-angles to the village street and faces south. Under its dilapidated thatch, it drowses in the sun behind a thorn hedge, causing cries of admiration from visitors who are charmed by the tiny diamond-paned windows and the ancient beams which criss-cross the brickwork.

'Pretty enough to look at from outside,' I tell them, 'but you wouldn't want to live there. All four riddled with damp, and there's no proper drainage.'

'I expect plenty of people lived happily enough in them, over the years,' they retort defensively, still dazzled by Tyler's Row's outer beauty. One tenant, years ago, trained the thorn hedge into an arch over the gateway, and this enhances the charm of the view beyond.

A brick path, rosy with age and streaked with moss, runs along the front of the row, and there are narrow flower borders beneath the windows. There's no doubt about it. On a fine summer's day, with the pansies turning up their kitten-faces to the sun, Tyler's Row makes a perfect subject for a 'Beautiful Britain' calendar. After a spell of drenching rain and wind, when the sagging thatch is dark with moisture, and the brick path is running with the rain from the roof, Tyler's Row looks what it is – a building fast reaching the end of its days unless something drastic is done to restore it.

Of course, as the besotted visitors point out, it has housed generations of Fairacre folk. Carters and ploughmen have brought up their families here – mother, father and the latest baby in one bedroom, girls in the other, and boys downstairs. Shepherds and shoe-menders, dress-makers and washerwomen, all have called Tyler's Row home over the years. At one time, at the end of Victoria's reign, there was even a poet beneath the thatch. He lived there alone, after his mother died, for many years, and the older people in Fairacre remember him.

Mr Willet, who is my school caretaker, sexton to St Patrick's, our parish church, and holder of a dozen or so important positions in our village, told me a little about him. The poor fellow had been christened Aloysius (locally pronounced as Loyshus), and was much given to reciting his works at local functions, if given half a chance.

'Lived to a great age, Loyshus did,' commented Mr Willet. 'Well, to tell you the truth, Miss Read, he didn't do much to wear himself out. That garden of his was like a jungle. The neighbours in Tyler's Row went on somethin' shockin' about it. No, he never put hisself out much. Never even bothered to wash hisself the last year or so. Smelt like a proper civet's paradise that house of his, when they finally came to clear up after him.'

Aloysius's poems are sometimes quoted in the *Caxley Chronicle*. In our part of the country, at least, a prophet is not without honour. Occasionally someone writes a short article about our local poet. The poems are pretty dreadful. He had a great fondness for apostrophes, and one of his better known works begins with the formidable lines:

> Ere e'en falls dewy o'er the dale,
> Mine eyes discern 'twixt glim and gloam

It goes on, if I remember rightly, for a hundred and sixty lines, with apostrophes scattered among them like a hatful of tadpoles.

'He were a holy terror at church socials,' recalls Mr Willet. 'Get old Loyshus on the platform, mumbling into his beard, and you could count on a good half-hour gettin' on with your game of noughts and crosses in the back row. 'Twere easy enough to get him up there, but gettin him down was murder. They took to putting him on just before the Glee Singers. They used to get so wild waitin' about sucking cough-drops ready for "When you Come Down The Vale, Love", that they fairly man-handled Loyshus back to his chair, as soon as he stopped to take a breath.'

'He sounds as though he was a problem,' I said.

'A problem, yes,' agreed Mr Willet, 'but then, you must remember, he was a *poet*. Bound to turn him funny, all that rhyming. We was half-sorry for Loyshus, really,' said Mr Willet tolerantly. 'I've met a sight of folk far worse than Loyshus. But not,' he added, with the air of one obliged to tell the truth, 'as smelly.'

When I first became head teacher at Fairacre School, Tyler's Row belonged to an old soldier called Jim Bennett. The rent for each cottage was three shillings a week, and had remained at this ridiculous sum for many years. With his twelve shillings a week income, poor Jim Bennett could do nothing in the way of repairs to his property, and he hated coming to collect his dues and to face the complaints of the tenants, most of whom were a great deal better off than he was himself.

The Coggs family lived in one cottage. Arthur Coggs was, and still is, the biggest ne'er-do-well in Fairacre, a drunkard and a bully. His wife and children had a particularly hard time of it when they lived at Tyler's Row. Joseph Coggs and his twin sisters frequently arrived at school hungry and in tears. Things seem a little better now that they have been moved to a council house.

The Waites lived next door, a bright, respectable family who also moved later into a council house.

An old couple, called John and Mary White, both as deaf as posts, sweet, vague and much liked in the village, occupied another cottage, and a waspish woman, named Mrs Fowler, lived at the last house. She was a trouble-maker, if ever there was one, and Jim Bennett quailed before the lash of her complaining tongue when he called for his modest dues.

The Coggs were moved out first, and an old comrade-in-arms, who had served in the Royal Horse Artillery with Jim Bennett in the First World War begged to be allowed to rent the house. Jim Bennett agreed readily. Sergeant Burnaby was old, and in poor health. His liver had suffered from the curries of India, when he had been stationed there, and bouts of malaria had added to the yellowness of his complexion. But he was upright and active, and managed his lone affairs very well.

The Waites moved and their cottage remained empty for some time, and then, soon afterwards the Whites grew too frail to manage for themselves, and went to live with a married daughter.

Now the two middle cottages of the row were empty, and Jim Bennett decided that it was as good a time as any to sell the property as a whole. Mrs Fowler at one end, and Sergeant Burnaby at the other, were not ideal tenants, and the fact that they were there at all must detract from the value of Tyler's Row, he knew well. But frankly, he had had enough of it, and he told his sister so.

They lived together at Beech Green in a cottage quite as inconvenient and dilapidated as any at Tyler's Row.

They sat on a wooden bench at the back of the house, in the hot July sunshine. The privet hedge was in flower, scenting the air with its cloying sweetness. Blackbirds fluted from the old plum tree, and gazed with bright, dark eyes at the blackcurrant bushes. Old white lace curtains had been prudently draped over them by Alice Bennett to protect the fruit from these marauders. From the plum tree they watched for an opportunity to overcome this challenge.

'We'll have to face it, Alice,' said Jim. 'The time's coming when we'll have to find a little place in Caxley – one of these old people's homes, something like that. If we sell up Tyler's Row we should have enough to see us pretty comfortable, with our pensions, until we snuff it.'

'You'll miss the rent,' said Alice.

Her brother laughed scornfully. 'A good miss, too! Traipsing out to Fairacre every week, to be growled at by Mrs Fowler, isn't my idea of pleasure. I'll be glad to see the back of Tyler's Row, and let someone else take it on.'

'Who'd want it,' asked Alice reasonably, 'with those two still there?'

'We'll see. I'm going into Caxley tomorrow to get Masters & Jones to put it on their books. Some young couple might be glad to knock a door between those middle cottages to make a real nice little house.'

'They won't fancy old Burnaby rapping on the wall one

side, and Mrs Vinegar Fowler on the other, if I know anything about it.'

'That's as may be. I'm getting too old to trouble about Tyler's Row. I'm content to take what the agents can get for it, and be shot of the responsibility.'

He knocked out his cherrywood pipe with finality. Alice, knowing when she was beaten, rose without a word, and went indoors to cut bread and butter for tea. Jim might be getting on for eighty, but there was no doubt he could still make up his mind.

And what was more, thought Alice, his decisions were usually right.

In no time at all it was common knowledge in Fairacre, Beech Green, and as far afield as the market town of Caxley, that Tyler's Row was up for sale. No advertisement had appeared, no sales board had been erected, but nevertheless everyone knew it for a fact.

The reasons given varied considerably. Some said that Mrs Fowler was buying it, having won several thousands from

a. the football pools

b. a tea competition

c. an appearance on a TV commercial advertisement.

('What for?' asked one wit. ' "Use our face cream, or else?" ')

Others held the view that the Sanitary People had condemned the property and it was going to be pulled down anyway.

Nearer the mark were those who guessed that Jim Bennett had had enough, and he was selling whilst there was a chance of making a few hundred.

The wildest theory of all was put forward by no less a person than the vicar, who was positive that he had heard that a society for the revival of Victorian poetry was buying the property, and proposed to open it to the public as a shrine to Aloysius's memory.

Certainly, within a week of the conversation between Jim and his sister in the privacy of their garden, everyone knew of the intended sale. He had told his tenants, of course, as soon as he had made up his mind, but they had said little. It was yet another case of air-borne gossip, so usual in a village as to be completely unremarkable.

Mrs Pringle, a glumly formidable dragon who keeps Fair-acre School clean, and who polishes the tortoise stoves with a ferocity which has to be seen to be believed, told me the news with her usual pessimism.

'So poor old Jim Bennett's having to sell Tyler's Row.'

'Is he?' I said, rising to the bait.

'Some say he's hard put to it to manage on his bit of pension, but I reckons there's more to it than that.'

There was a smugness about the way Mrs Pringle pulled in her three chins, and the purse of her downward-curving mouth which told me that I should hear more.

She put a pudgy hand on my desk and leant forward to address me conspiratorially. 'It's my belief he's Got Something. Something the doctors can't do anything about.'

'Oh, *really* . . .' I began impatiently, but was swept aside.

'Mark my words, Jim Bennett knows his Time Has Come, and he's putting his affairs in order. By the time that sales board goes up, we'll know the worst, no doubt.'

An expression of the utmost satisfaction spread ever her face, and she made for the lobby with never a trace of a limp – a sure sign that, for once in her martyred existence, Mrs Pringle was enjoying life.

2. PROSPECTIVE BUYERS

But, amazingly, the board did not go up. While Fairacre speculated upon this, the firm of estate agents in Caxley had informed several clients already seeking country houses that Tyler's Row was now for sale, and they enclosed glowing reports on the desirability of the property.

Among those who received a letter from Masters & Jones was Peter Hale, a schoolmaster in his fifties. He sat at his breakfast table, toast in one hand, the letter in the other and read hastily through the half-glasses on the end of his nose.

Every now and again he glanced at the clock on the mantel-piece. At half-past eight every morning of term time, for just over thirty years, Peter Hale had set off down the hill to Caxley Grammar School where he taught mathematics and history to the lower forms.

He walked the half-mile or so regularly, for the good of his health. As a young man he had been a sprinter and a hurdler, and the thought of losing his athletic figure, as so many of his fellow colleagues had done, was anathema to him. To tell the truth, exercise was something of a fetish with Peter Hale, and his family and friends were sometimes amused, sometimes irritated, by his earnest recommendations of a 'good five-mile walk', or 'a run before breakfast' for any minor illnesses, ranging from a cold in the head to a wasp sting. His wife declared that he had once advised one of these sovereign remedies for her sprained ankle. It might just have been possible.

She was a small, plump, pretty woman with a complexion like a peach. Once fair, her hair was now silvery-grey and softly curled. She was very little changed from the girl Peter had met and married within a year. There was a gentle vagueness about her which won most people's affection. The less charitable dismissed Diana Hale as 'rather bird-brained', which she most certainly was not. Beneath the feminine softness and the endearing good manners was a quick intelligence. Her anxiety not to hurt people kept her sharpness sheathed like a sword in its scabbard; bur it was there, nevertheless, and this awareness of the ridiculous and the incongruous gave her much secret amusement.

The clock said twenty-five past eight and Diana waited for the last quick gulp of coffee and the rolling of her husband's table napkin.

He tossed the letter across to her, and lifted his cup. 'What do you think of it? Shall we go and have a look?'

'Fairacre,' said Diana slowly. 'Wouldn't it be rather far?'

'Six miles or so. Not much more. And lovely country – good downland walks. High too. Wonderful air.'

Peter Hale tucked his spectacles into their case, checked that he had his red marking pen safely in his inner pocket, his handkerchief in another and his wallet in the back pocket of his trousers. 'So much more convenient for the pickpockets,' as Diana had told him once.

'Must be off. I'll be late back. Staff meeting after school.'

He gave her forehead a quick peck, and was gone.

Diana poured a second cup of coffee and thought about this proposed move. She wasn't at all sure that she wanted to move anyway. They had lived in the present house for almost twenty years and she had grown very attached to it.

It had been built early in the century, in common with many others, on the hill south of Caxley. Mostly they had been taken by professional and business people in the town, who wanted to move away from their working premises, yet did not want to be too far off.

They were well built, with ample gardens whose trees were now mature and formed a screen against the increased traffic in the road. Diana had worked hard in the garden, scrapping the enormous herbaceous border which had been the pride of a full-time gardener in earlier and more affluent times, and the dozen or so geometrically-shaped garden beds which had been so beautifully set out with wallflowers, and then geraniums, in days gone by.

The two long rose beds were her own creation, and a new shrubbery, well planted with bulbs, gave her much satisfaction and less backbreaking work. She would hate to leave her handiwork to others.

The house too, though originally built with accommodation for at least one resident maid, was easily managed. Here she and Peter had brought up their two sons, both now in the Navy, and the place was full of memories.

And Caxley itself was dear to her. She enjoyed shopping in the town, meeting her friends for coffee, hearing the news of their sons and daughters, taking part in such innocent and agreeable activities as the Operatic Society and the Floral Club. Her nature made her averse to committee work. She lacked the drive and concentration needed, and had never been able to whip up the moral indignation she witnessed in some of her friends who were engaged in public works. She admired their zeal sincerely, but she knew she was incapable of emulating them.

She knew so many people in the town. After all, Peter was now teaching the sons of his former pupils, and every family, it seemed, had some tie with the Grammar School. The young men in the banks, the shops and the offices of Caxley were almost all Old Boys, and knew her well. Wouldn't she feel lost at Fairacre?

She told herself reasonably that she would still run into Caxley to shop and meet friends, but it would mean a second car. She knew that any buses from Fairacre would be few and far between. Had Peter considered this, she wondered, in his desire to get into the country?

He had wanted to do this for years now. Circumstances had kept them in the town, the boys' schooling, the convenience of being within walking distance of his work, and Diana's obvious contentment with her way of life. But the boys were now out in the world. The house was really too large for them, and the garden, with no help available, was soon going to prove too much for them.

'Now's the time to pull up our roots,' Peter had said, at least a year earlier. 'We're still young and active enough to settle into another place and to make friends. I'd like to get well dug in before I retire.' He looked at his wife's doubtful face. 'If we don't go soon, we never will,' he said flatly. 'It's time we had a change of scene. Let's go and look at a few places anyway.'

During the past few months they had visited a dozen or so properties, and each time they had returned thankfully to their own home.

At this time, estate agents could laud their wares to the skies and many a 'desirable residence in charming surroundings' could have been more truthfully described as 'Four walls and a roof in a wilderness'. Sometimes, it was enough to read the agent's description, and the Hales did not bother to visit the establishment. Other factors weeded out the possibles from the impossibles. For instance, Peter Hale refused to have any-thing to do with a property advertised ' 'twixt' this and that, or as 'prestige'.

'Listen to this,' he would snap crossly. ' " 'Twixt downs and salubrious golf course." And here's another, even worse. "A gem set 'twixt wood and weir." Well, they're out for a start! I'm not living 'twixt anything.'

There would be further snorts of disgust.

'It says here that "Four prestige houses are planned in Elderberry Lane". Such idiotic phrases! And pandering to the vanity of silly people! Who's going to be gulled into thinking Elderberry Lane's any catch, anyway, stuck down by the gas-works?'

They knew the district well after so many years, and Fair-acre was one of the villages which attracted them. In open country leading to the downs, it remained relatively unspoilt, yet there were one or two useful shops, a Post Office, a fine church, and enough inhabitants to make life interesting.

'This might be a possibility,' said Diana to herself, studying the glowing account of Tyler's Row's attractions.

'Suitable for conversion into one dignified residence', prob-ably meant it was falling down and needed prompt support internally and externally.

'Half an acre of mature garden' could be construed as two ancient plum trees, past bearing, standing among docks and stinging nettles, and 'leaded windows' would be the deuce to clean, thought Diana.

But the price was unusually low. Why, she wondered? Was it even more dilapidated than she imagined?

And then she saw the snag. 'Two of the cottages at present occupied.' Hardly worth bothering to go and look then. They certainly wouldn't want neighbours at such close quarters.

'Still,' thought Diana reasonably, 'it does mean that the cottages are capable of being lived in.'

Perhaps they would run out to Fairacre after all.

*

As it happened, the Hales did not visit Fairacre until the following week, for end of term was upon them, involving Sports Day, a tennis tournament arranged by the hard-working Parents' Association to raise funds for the school's new swimming pool, a dinner for three of the staff who were retiring, as well as the usual end-of-term chores such as reports, last-minute advice to panicking school-leavers looking for jobs, and so on.

'Well,' said Peter Hale, arriving home on the last day of term, with a broad smile, 'now we've broken up, and my peptic ulcers can recover gently.' He flopped into the settee, put up his feet and surveyed the ceiling blissfully. 'Think of it – seven weeks of freedom. Time to do just as we like.'

'If you still want to look at that place at Fairacre, perhaps we could drive out tomorrow,' suggested Diana.

'Tomorrow, the day after, the day after that, any day you like, my dear. I'm a free man,' declared Peter rapturously.

'If we leave it too long,' pointed out his wife, 'it will have been snapped up.'

'So it might,' agreed her husband, coming abruptly to earth. 'Let's go tomorrow morning.'

It was a perfect day to drive the six miles northward to Fairacre. They picked up the key as they drove through Caxley, and were soon out of the town, driving through leafy lanes, and rising steadily as they approached the downs.

The sky was cloudless, and a blue haze shimmered over the wide fields. Honeysuckle and a few late wild roses embroidered the hedges, and when Peter stopped the car to fill his pipe, Diana heard a lark scattering its song from the sky. A blue butterfly, native of the chalk country, hovered over the purple knapweed on the bank. Nearby was a patch of yellow and cream toadflax, vivid in the sunshine, and everywhere was the scent of warm grass and leaves – the very essence of summertime.

'Wonderful country,' said Peter dreamily, gazing into the blue distance, above the leaping match flame.

'In this weather,' replied Diana. 'Could be pretty bleak in the winter. And lonely.'

'You don't sound very enthusiastic,' said Peter, turning to look at her. 'Shall we go back?'

'Not till we've seen Tyler's Row,' said Diana firmly. 'We'll know what to think then.'

Peter started the engine and they made their way slowly through Beech Green and on to Fairacre, without speaking further, until they reached the Post Office in the centre of the village street.

As it happened, Mr Lamb, the postmaster, was in his front garden, cutting back rose suckers with a fierce-looking clasp knife.

'Tyler's Row?' called Peter, winding down the car window.

'Eh?' said Mr Lamb, startled.

'Tyler's Row – Mr Bennett's property,' enlarged Peter, knowing that it is far better to name the owner than the house in rural parts.

John Lamb, who had not heard Peter properly at first, was a trifle nettled at having Bennett's name brought in. He was postmaster, wasn't he? He knew Tyler's Row well enough, after all these years, without some foreigner trying to tell him his business!

He answered rather shortly.

'On your left. Matter of a hundred yards or so. You'll see the thatch over the hedge-top.'

'Thanks very much,' said Peter, equally shortly.

Diana turned her gentle smile upon John Lamb, to soften her husband's brusqueness.

'Surly sort of devil,' commented Peter, eyes alert to the left.

'I thought he looked rather a dear,' said Diana. 'Look, that's it!'

They pulled up by the tall hawthorn hedge.

'That archway's rather attractive,' said Diana. 'Shall we go in?'

The gate was rickety and dragged on the ground. A semi-circle had been worn into the earth, and the pressure had caused some of the palings to hang loose.

'Tut, tut!' clicked Peter, who was a tidy man. 'Only the hinge gone. Wouldn't have taken five minutes to replace.'

They stood just inside the gate and surveyed Tyler's Row. The cottage nearest them had a fine yellow rose climbing over it. The dark foliage glittered in the sunshine as brightly as holly leaves. The windows were closely shut, despite the heat of the day, and Diana was positive that she saw a curtain twitch as though someone were watching them.

They moved a few steps along the brick path. A bumble bee wandered lazily from rose to rose, his humming adding to the general air of languor.

The two empty cottages, their windows blank and curtain-less, looked forlorn and unloved. The paint peeled from the doors and window frames, and a long, skinny branch of japonica blew gently back and forth in the light breeze, scraping across the glass of an upstairs window with an irritating squeaking noise.

'Turns your teeth to chalk, doesn't it?' remarked Peter, 'Like catching your finger-nail on the blackboard.'

'Or wearing those crunchy nylon gloves,' added Diana.

'I've been spared that,' said Peter, stepping forward and pressing his face to the glass.

At that moment, a woman came out of the last cottage, flung a bucket of water across the garden bed, in a flashing arc, and stood, hand on hip, surveying the couple. Her face was grim, her eyes unwelcoming.

'Can I help?' she asked tartly. It looked as though it were the last thing she wanted to do, but Diana answered her softly.

'No, thank you. We'll try not to bother you. We have the key to look at these cottages.'

At the same moment, the door of the other occupied cottage opened, and out stepped Sergeant Burnaby. His face was as yellow as his roses, but his bearing was still soldierly.

'Yes, sir,' he said briskly. 'Anything I can do to help, sir?'

'Nothing, thanks,' said Peter, with a smile. 'Just taking a look at the property.'

'In a very poor way, sir. Very poor way indeed. My old friend Jim Bennett hasn't the wherewithal to keep it together. No discredit to him. Just circumstances, you understand. A fine man he is, sir. We served together for –'

A violent snort from the woman at the end interrupted the old soldier's monologue, and Peter Hale took the opportunity of turning the key in the lock and opening the door of one of the cottages.

'We mustn't keep you,' he said firmly and, ushering Diana inside, he closed the door upon the two remaining tenants of Tyler's Row.

Despite the summer heat which throbbed over the garden, the cottage interior was cold and damp. This was the Waites' old home, and had been empty now for a long time. Cobwebs draped the windows and a finger of ivy had crept inside and was feeling its way up the crack of the door. Diana could smell the bruised aromatic scent where the opening door had grazed it.

The floor was of uneven bricks, and snails had left their silver trails across it. The old-fashioned kitchen range was mottled with rust, and some soot had spattered from the chimney to the hearth.

But the room was unusually large, with a window back and front, and there were several fine oak beams across the low ceiling. There were two more doors. One opened upon a narrow staircase, and the other led to a smaller room.

Above stairs were two fair-sized bedrooms, and the view at the back of the cottage was breath-taking. Mile upon mile, it seemed, of cornfields, just beginning to be tinged with gold, stretched away to the summit of the downs. A hawk hovered nearby, a motionless speck in the clear blue, and from everywhere, it seemed to Diana, came the sound of larks singing.

She forced open one of the creaking windows, and the sweet air lifted her hair. Peter came behind her, and they gazed together in silence.

Immediately below them lay the four long, narrow gardens. Sergeant Burnaby's had a row of runner beans growing in it, and a strip of bright annuals, poppies, cornflowers, marigolds and nasturtiums, growing higgledy-piggledy together near the back door.

A ramshackle run containing half a dozen hens and a splendid cockerel completed Sergeant Burnaby's garden, with the exception of a stout wooden armchair, much weather-beaten, that stood on the flagstones in the shelter of the house.

Mrs Fowler's garden had a concrete windmill, two stone ducks, a frog twice as large as the ducks, and a neat rose bed planted with a dozen standard roses. Beyond this stretched the kitchen garden, ruled neatly into rows of onions, beet-root, parsnips, carrots, and a positive sea of flourishing potato plants. A clothes-line, near the house, bore a row of fiercely white tea-towels and pillow-cases which Diana guessed, correctly, had been bleached within an inch of their lives.

Between the two gardens lay the wide, neglected area of grass, docks and nettles which Diana had envisaged. There seemed to be a square of fruit bushes, almost shrouded in weeds, towards the end of one garden, and a rustic arch leant, like the Tower of Pisa, halfway down the other. It was a sad scene of desolation, but for some reason it did not depress Diana. Her gardener's heart was touched at the sight of so much neglect, but unaccountably she wanted to shout from the window to the beleaguered plants, telling them to hang on, to cling to life, that help was coming, that she would save them.

She was surprised, and slightly amused, at the vehemence of the feeling which shook her. She was becoming bewitched!

Peter was now stamping on the ancient floorboards, which stood up to this onslaught sturdily. His eyes scrutinized the beams for woodworm, his fingernails peeled a little of the damp wallpaper, and he sniffed the air, like a pointer, for any trace of dry rot. They went down the squeaking stairs and into the next cottage. It was a replica of the first, with another large room adjoining a small one, and two bedrooms above, but the staircase here was broken and dangerously splintered, and the dampness, if anything, more noticeable.

'What do you think?' asked Diana.

'Humph!' grunted her husband enigmatically.

'Do you want to look at the other two? I suppose we can?'

'Not now, anyway. I've seen enough, I think. Let's go back and think about it.'

There was no sign of Mrs Fowler or Sergeant Burnaby as they closed and locked the doors, but martial music was issuing loudly from the latter's radio set and competed with the humming of insects enjoying the downland sunshine.

They closed the broken gate carefully, and looked through the archway at the scene which had fascinated so many sightseers before them.

'It would never do, of course,' said Diana, at last. 'Although it's a heavenly spot –' Her voice trailed away.

Despite her words, she had the odd feeling that the forlorn cottages and the smothered garden were beseeching her for help. Could she withstand that piteous cry?

'I need my tea,' she said forcefully, turning her back upon Tyler's Row.

She made her way, almost in panic, it seemed to her surprised husband, back to the haven of the car.

3. LOCAL COMPETITORS

The Hales, of course, were not the only people to visit Tyler's Row, and as the village watched the callers, speculation grew animated.

'One chap came from Lincolnshire,' said Mr Willet. 'Said he knew these parts from the fishing, and might retire here. I met him outside The Beetle. Very civil-spoken, he was, too, coming from so far away.'

Mr Willet spoke as though this were extremely odd, as if Lincolnshire people might be expected to have their heads growing from their breasts, like the natives described by medieval travellers in distant lands.

But most of the visitors came from Caxley or neighbouring villages. One indeed came from Fairacre itself, and he was Henry Mawne.

Henry Mawne and his wife have lived in Fairacre for some time. He is a renowned ornithologist, but better known in our village as a zealous churchwarden and parish councillor. He and his wife occupy part of a fine Queen Anne house at the end of the village. Why should he want to move?

'Finding them stairs too much, I don't doubt,' said one.

'Needs more room for all them books and papers of his,' said another.

'Wants his own home, I expect,' said a third. 'Who wants to die in a rented place?'

As it happened, all three reasons had something to do with Mr Mawne's interest in Tyler's Row. Both he and his wife had twinges of arthritis, and the idea of making a home on the ground floor appealed to them.

Then, their present abode was some distance from the hub of the village. The Post Office, the shops, the church, and the bus stop were close to Tyler's Row. And his books grew more numerous as the years passed and, despite his wife's threats to throw them out, Henry Mawne refused to part with a single volume. At least one room downstairs could be set aside as a library-cum-office, and the lesser-used books could be housed upstairs.

And then, Tyler's Row had always attracted him. The long thatched roof, silvery with age, its southern-facing aspect, making it bask like a cat in the sunshine, its thick hawthorn hedge screening it from the road, had all combined to delight Henry Mawne whenever he passed the property.

His wife was less kindly disposed. A forthright woman, who has upset many a Fairacre worthy with her bluntness, she told her husband just what she thought of the project.

'Nothing but a hovel, and those two old people a positive menace. There's nothing wrong with this present place, except the stairs and your books. We can still manage the first, and if you would only weed out the second we should be perfectly happy.'

Henry Mawne doubted this privately, but had the sense to hold his tongue. He dropped the argument for the time being, but returned to it several times in the next few days, for it was a matter which obsessed him.

His wife remained adamant, but was beginning to realize that she was up against unusually stubborn opposition. Henry Mawne had been back and forth to the estate agent's and to Tyler's Row, and had even gone so far as to get the place surveyed.

'You see, my dear,' he told his wife, 'this might be an investment. It is ridiculously cheap because of the tenants and the dilapidation. I know we should have to spend a lot on it, but we've enough behind us to cope with it. We could make a start on the empty pair, making them one, and let it when it was done, until we felt we wanted to move in ourselves.'

'You mean, stay here indefinitely?' asked his wife suspiciously.

'I don't see why not. We should be on the spot for watching

the building's progress, and as you say we can manage here for some time yet.'

'I'll think about it,' said Mrs Mawne cautiously.

'Well, think quickly,' adjured her husband. 'There are other people interested in Tyler's Row.'

But his heart leapt, nevertheless, at this tiny chink in his wife's armour. Dare he hope?

Much the same debate was going on at the Hales' house. The comparative cheapness of the property appealed particularly to Peter, for schoolmasters are usually hard up and this seemed to be a sound investment.

'The site alone is worth best part of the money,' he told his wife. 'Plots of land fetch astronomical prices now round here. We should get a good price for this place, and it would be comforting to have something in the bank. We'll be down to half our income when I retire. We must look ahead.'

'I know that,' answered Diana unhappily, 'but I really think that we shall find those two old things a terrible headache. If we could be sure they would be leaving soon –'

'If Nature takes its course properly they'll be leaving in the next year or two. That old soldier is truly in the sere and yellow. I doubt if he'll last the winter.'

'Don't be so horribly calculating.'

'Who started it?'

'I didn't so much mean *dying* –' began Diana, prevaricating.

'Well, they're not likely to move out just to oblige us,' said Peter flatly. 'They're fixtures all right, and we shall have to face the fact.'

'I hate being hustled,' said Diana, changing her tactics.

'Me too. I don't propose to leave this place until the next is habitable. That's understood. But if we made up our minds now, I could spend quite a bit of time during the summer holidays going over plans with the architect, and doing a certain amount myself.'

'I do see that, but oh dear!' sighed Diana.

'Look at it this way,' said Peter, pressing home the attack. 'It's nearer the mark than anything else we've seen so far. We've always liked Fairacre. It's only twenty minutes from Caxley, and the site of the house is perfect. Faces south, just enough garden, endless possibilities with the whole row to consider –'

'You sound like Masters & Jones rolled into one. Are you sure you're not being too optimistic?'

'Are you sure you're not being downright awkward?' retaliated Peter. 'What, in heaven's name, beside the two tenants, have you got against the place?'

'It's dark. It's damp. It's falling down.'

'So was that mill house the Kings bought ten years ago. When I went to see it with him, a mother rat the size of a rhino met us at the front door, with about twenty-five babies tagging along behind. Now it's superb, and would sell for a bomb. Tyler's Row could be even better than that.'

'If I could be *sure*', said Diana slowly, 'that the middle part would be absolutely ready to move into, and that there was some possibility of those two going in a reasonable time, so that we could incorporate their cottages eventually, then I think I'd agree.' Her face lit up, as an idea struck her. 'Couldn't we offer them alternative accommodation? I'm sure I've heard something about it.'

'They'd have to be willing to go, and you know what it's like finding something suitable. Still, I could find out about it.'

'Give me until tomorrow to get used to the idea,' said Diana. 'I think making decisions is the most exhausting thing in the world.'

'You want practice,' commented her husband drily.

Diana woke at two o'clock in the morning, the problem still unresolved. She had gone over the pros and cons so many times that her head buzzed.

In the other bed Peter snored rhythmically. Moonlight flooded the room, and an owl's cry wavered from the trees which edged the common some quarter of a mile away.

Diana lay there, savouring the quietness. It would be quieter still at Fairacre, she supposed, remembering the vast sweep of downs behind the village.

The remembrance of the neglected garden in the foreground flooded back to her, and she was shaken, yet again, by the longing to rescue it from decay. It could be so lovely in that setting, and the soil was rich, as the fine plants in the neighbours' gardens proved. Pinks should do well on that chalky soil, and lavender. A lavender hedge would grow easily . . .

Her mind drifted vaguely, and then came back to Peter. It was only fair that he should have his way in this matter. For years he had put up with Caxley for the sake of the family, always longing to settle eventually in the countryside nearby. This was their chance.

Diana sighed, and decided to creep downstairs to warm some milk. It might make her sleep. Experience told her that nothing short of clashing cymbals would stir Peter from his rest, but nevertheless, she went on tiptoe from the room and down the stairs. The moonlight was so bright that there was no need to switch on lights until she entered the kitchen.

The cat gave a welcoming chirrup, stretched luxuriously, and descended from its bed on the kitchen chair near the stove. It watched Diana expectantly as she poured milk into a saucepan. A little snack in the middle of the night never came amiss.

Diana shared the milk between her mug and the cat's saucer, and stood warming her hands as she sipped.

'How'd you like to live in the country, puss?' asked Diana, watching the pink tongue at work. But the cat, strangely enough, never answered questions, and Diana carried her mug and her problems back to bed.

'Go ahead,' she said next morning, when Peter awoke.

'Go ahead where?'

'With the house.'

'The Fairacre one?'

'What else?' said Diana, slightly nettled. Peter never came to full consciousness until after breakfast. This morning he seemed more comatose than usual.

'You're sure?'

'No, I'm not, but I think we could make something of it, and if we're going to move, then now's the right time.'

There was silence for a time, and then Diana heard humming from the other bed, proving that her husband was feeling contented. It was difficult to recognize the tune. It might have been 'Onward Christian Soldiers', 'Take a Pair of Sparkling Eyes' roughly transposed for a tuneless baritone, or possibly the marching music from 'Dr Zhivago'. Peter's repertoire was limited, but gave him a great deal of private pleasure, and Diana a keen appreciation of variations on several themes.

'Better get up, then,' said Peter, throwing aside the bed-clothes. 'I'll get down to Masters & Jones as soon as they open.'

Still humming – the Dr Zhivago motif coming through strongly now – he made his way to the bathroom.

Masters & Jones estate agents' office presented a fine Georgian front, all red brick and white-painted sash windows, to Caxley High Street. It looked what it was, a long-established prosperous family business which had served Caxley and its neighbourhood well for four generations. William Masters had founded the firm in the year of the Great Exhibition of 1851, and three of his descendants were still active in the firm. Clough Jones, a foreigner from Pontypool, joined the firm in 1920, and so was a comparative newcomer to Caxley. His beautiful tenor voice was soon taking the lead in Caxley's

Operatic Society and he was reckoned to be 'a very steady sort of chap'. Some added 'for a Welshman' in the year or two after Clough's arrival, but this proviso was soon dropped – proof that he had shown his worth.

Peter had taught two of the Masters' boys and Clough's only son Ellis. It was the younger of the Masters' boys, now a man of twenty-eight, who welcomed Peter to the office and set a chair for him on the other side of the desk.

The interior of the house was disappointing. The large square rooms on each side of the hall had been divided into four, with partitions of flimsy wood topped with reeded glass. Occasionally one would catch sight of a head, curiously distorted, in the next compartment, elongated like a giraffe-woman from Africa, or bulging sideways like a squashed Christmas pudding, according to the angle of the glass through which it was visible.

The floors were covered with linoleum of a pattern purporting to be wood blocks. As these were of such unlikely colours as pale blue, orange and pink, the effect was unconvincing, and to Peter, eyeing it distastefully, thoroughly shocking.

'Very nice to see you, sir,' said young Masters deferentially. It seemed only yesterday that he was waiting outside the detention room door under Mr Hales' stern direction. Something to do with the unification of Germany and Italy, if he remembered correctly, had brought him to that pretty pass, and now he came to think of it, he was still not much wiser on the subject, detention or no detention. But he had always felt a healthy respect for old Hale, and even now a slight tremor affected his knees at the thought of past bondage.

'I've come about this property at Fairacre,' said Peter. He looked over his spectacles at the young man. David, Paul, John? What the deuce was the boy called?

'Can't remember your name, I'm afraid,' he added.

'Philip, sir.'

'Ah, yes, Philip. Second fifteen full back.'

'No, sir. That was my brother Jack. I wasn't much good.'

'Forget my own name next,' replied Peter cheerfully. 'Well, I'm thinking of going ahead with Tyler's Row. Better have a survey. Sooner the better.'

'Yes, indeed,' said Philip, with more confidence. 'You will certainly need to get moving, sir. Another gentleman is being rather pressing.'

Peter Hale looked sternly across his spectacles. 'Is this the truth?'

Philip was instantly transformed into a wrong-doing first-former, despite his six feet in height.

'Yes, sir. Honestly, sir,' he heard himself saying nervously. Heavens above, his voice seemed to have become treble again! He took a grip upon himself, and cleared his throat. Dammit, this was his office, wasn't it? 'A gentleman already resident in Fairacre –'

' "Living in" or "residing", if you must,' corrected Peter automatically.

Philip, clinging to his precarious confidence, ignored the interruption. 'He is very interested in the property and has already had it surveyed. I think it's quite likely he will make us an offer. Probably in advance of the selling price.'

'More fool him,' said Peter flatly. 'I'm not bribing anybody.'

'Of course not, sir. But I should advise you to get a survey done immediately. I could go out myself.'

'Do that then, Philip, will you?'

'I'll just jot down one or two reminders.'

He pulled a sheet of paper towards him and began to scribble diligently with his left hand.

Terrible writing that boy always did have, remembered Peter, watching his old pupil at work. Felt sure he'd be a doctor with that scrawl, but not enough brains really, nice fellow though he was. He looked at the bent head, the beautifully clean white parting, the well-shaven cheeks, and felt a warm glow. Should be able to trust him – solid chap, nice family, respectable firm. Why, young Philip might bring Tyler's Row to him eventually! He was smiling when the young man looked up.

'You'd be happy there, sir,' he said, stating a fact, not asking a question.

'I think we should,' agreed Peter.

He rose and went to the door, his gaze on the linoleum. 'Who chose this?' he asked, pointing a toe.

'I did, sir,' said Philip proudly.

'Pity,' said Peter, in farewell.

4. MRS PRINGLE SMELLS TROUBLE

Who was to be the new owner of Tyler's Row? This was the question which exercised the whole of Fairacre.

Henry Mawne had been the favourite for so long that it was something of a shock to learn that he had retired from the race, and that an outsider was the winner.

The news came to me from Mrs Pringle during the summer holidays. She spends one morning each week 'putting me to rights', as she says, and although her presence is more of a penance than a pleasure, the results of her hard work are excellent. I try to do any of my simple entertaining on Wednesday evenings. It is the one day in the week when the place really shines.

'That sitting-room of yours wants bottoming,' said Mrs Pringle dourly. This, construed, meant that a thorough springcleaning was considered necessary.

'Looks all right to me,' I replied, quailing inwardly. Mrs Pringle bottoming anything is one of the major forces of nature, something between a volcano and a hurricane, and certainly frightening and uncomfortable.

'Seems to me you just lays a duster round when you feel like it. That side table's a fair disgrace, all over hot rings where you've put down your cup, and ink spots no honest woman could get off.'

'Well, I sometimes –' I began, but was swept aside. The hurricane was gaining force nicely.

'Mrs Hope, poor soul that she was, was a stickler for doing the furniture right. Every piece was gone over once a week with a nice piece of soft cloth wrung out in warm water and vinegar.'

When Mrs Hope's example is invoked I know that I may as well give in. She lived in the school house many years ago. Her husband is remembered as an unsuccessful poet who drowned his sorrows in drink, and was finally asked to leave. But Mrs Hope has left behind her a reputation for cleanliness as fierce and unremitting as Mrs Pringle's own.

'Mrs Hope didn't have to teach all day,' I said, putting up a poor defence.

'*Mrs Hope*,' boomed Mrs Pringle, 'would have kept her place clean *and* taut! Nothing slipshod about Mrs Hope.'

'You win,' I said resignedly. 'Shall I make coffee now?'

Mrs Pringle inclined her head graciously. 'And put it on a tray. I've enough marks to rub orf the table as it is.'

Over coffee, she told me the news.

'Mrs Mawne put her foot down, so I hear. Never liked the idea of moving so Mrs Willet said. Her sister was doing a bit of ewfolstery for her –'

'A bit of *what*?'

'Ewfolstery. Covering chairs, and couches and such-like. Well, as I was saying, Mrs Mawne told her plain that they had looked at Tyler's Row and decided against it. *She'd* decided,

she meant! Anyone could see the poor old gent would have loved it.'

'So it's on the market still?'

Mrs Pringle swelled with the gratified pride of one about to impart secret knowledge.

'I've been told – by One Who Should Know – that Mr Hale from the Grammar School's having it.'

'Probably just rumour,' I said off-handedly. A cunning move this, to learn more, but I still smarted under the threat of being bottomed.

Mrs Pringle rose to the bait beautifully. Her wattles turned red, and wobbled with all the fury of an enraged turkey-cock.

'My John's sister-in-law cleans at Masters & Jones and she's seen Mr Hale in and out of that place like a whirligig! And what's more, he's been to Tyler's Row hisself nigh on half-a-dozen times in the last fortnight, fair bristling with foot-rules and pencils and papers. He's having it all right, mark my words!'

'Well, well! We'll have to wait and see, won't we?' I said, with just a nice touch of disbelief. 'Anyway, he'd be a pleasant neighbour.'

'*Respectable*,' agreed Mrs Pringle, accepting a second Garibaldi biscuit graciously. 'Friendly, too, they say. Though he fair lays about those boys, from what my nephew says, if they don't work.'

'I'm glad to hear it,' I said. 'He sounds a man after my own heart. When's he coming?'

'You tell me!' replied Mrs Pringle emphatically. 'He's got an architect *and* a builder, so between 'em both that'll hold thing's up. The architect was out doin' what Mr Willet tells me is a survey, though he saw young Masters doing one too, a week or so back. Shows he's serious, doesn't it? Having two people to look at it, I mean?'

She dusted a crumb or two from her massive bosom, and rose to continue her labours.

'If he's in by next spring, he'll be lucky,' she foretold gloomily. 'And then I wish him joy of his neighbours, poor soul.'

I must confess that the future of Tyler's Row did not concern me greatly, although I have as keen an interest in village affairs, I think, as most people in Fairacre.

But I had troubles of my own at this time. As well as the intimidating prospect of Mrs Pringle's bottoming in the near future, I was also threatened with the formation of a Parent–Teacher Association at Fairacre School.

For generations any association between parents and teachers has been a natural one – sometimes enthusiastically co-operative, sometimes acrimonious, according to circumstances. But always it has been of an informal type – and it has worked very well.

I don't mind admitting that I am a non-committee woman. The very sight of an agenda fills me with dreadful boredom, and all that jargon about 'delegating authority to a sub-committee', and 'forwarding resolutions' to this and that, renders me numb and vague. The thought of an association which met once a month and involved speakers and demonstrations, and general sociability, filled me with depression. It would mean yet another evening away from my snug fireside, sitting in the draughty schoolroom and acting as reluctant hostess to a bevy of parents whom I saw quite enough of, in any case.

The moving force behind this sudden activity was a newcomer to the village, Mrs Johnson. The family had moved into a cottage in the village street once occupied by a lovable slattern called Mrs Emery and her family. Mr Emery had worked at an establishment, some miles away, known to us as 'the Atomic'. Mr Johnson also worked there, and was a somewhat pompous young man of left-ish tendencies, who had some difficulty in finding cruel masters grinding the faces of the poor, but lived in hope.

His wife, rather more militant, held strong views on education. She brought three young sons to the school soon after the summer term started. They were pale, bespectacled children, fiercely articulate, in contrast to my normal placid pupils, but quite amenable and keen to work. We got on very well.

But their mother was a sore trial. She met them at the school gate every afternoon, and button-holed me. I was subjected to tirades of information – usually faulty – on such topics as the dangers of formal teaching, the necessity for monthly intelligence tests, absolute freedom of thought, word and deed for each child and, of course, the complete rebuilding of Fairacre school.

There are very few teachers who welcome this sort of thing at four o'clock in the afternoon after a hard day's teaching. My civility soon grew thin, and I was obliged to tell her that any complaints must be dealt with at an appointed time. After this, I had fewer face-to-face encounters at the gate, but a number of letters, badly typed on flimsy paper and running to three or four pages, setting forth half-baked theories on education bearing no relevance, that I could see, upon present circumstances.

Unfortunately, Mrs Johnson and Mrs Mawne became close friends, and Mrs Mawne is one of the school's managers.

Whether she was still smarting from the wounds inflicted in the battle of Tyler's Row, from which she had emerged the victor, I shall never know. But certainly, soon after Mrs Pringle's conversation, the pressure for the formation of a Parent–Teacher Association was intensified. The vicar, who is chairman of the managers, mentioned the matter on several occasions.

'I really think it is unnecessary,' I told him, yet again. 'Fairacre's managed very well without one, and it's going to be a real headache finding something to do regularly every month, or whenever it is proposed to meet. If I felt that the majority of parents wanted it, then I'd submit with good grace, but I feel sure Mrs Johnson's at the bottom of this, and I don't suppose that family will stay in the village any longer than the Emerys did. I give them two years at the most.'

The poor vicar looked unhappy.

'We have a managers' meeting tomorrow, and this is one of the matters to be discussed, as you know.'

I did not, as a matter of fact, as the notice had been thrust, unread, behind the clock on the mantelpiece from whence I should snatch it one minute before the meeting.

'Do consider it, my dear Miss Read,' said the vicar, his kind old face puckered with anxiety. 'And what does Mrs Bonny think about it?'

I realized, with a shock, that I had never even thought of consulting Mrs Bonny, the infants' teacher, about this possibility. This was remiss of me, and I must put the matter right without delay.

When the vicar had gone, his cloak swirling in the fresh summer breeze from the downs, I made my way to the infants' room where Mrs Bonny was walking among her charges' desks, admiring plasticine baskets of fruit, crayoned portraits of each other, notable for rows of teeth like piano keys, and inordinately long necklaces of wooden beads which trailed over the desks like exotic knobbly snakes. It was a peaceful scene, and Mrs Bonny, a plump pink widow in her fifties, added to the air of cosiness.

'Very nice,' I said, to an upheld blue banana.

'Beautiful,' I said, to a picture executed by one of the Coggs' twins, showing her sister with one mauve eye, one yellow, and a mop of what appeared to be scarlet steel wool at the top of the portrait.

By this time, every piece of work in the room was raised for my inspection and approval.

'Wonderful! Very good effort! Lovely beads! Neat work! You have tried hard!'

The comments rattled out as evenly as peas from a shooter. Then I clapped my hands, and told them to continue.

'Sweets for quiet workers,' I added, resorting to a little bribery.

'The vicar's been talking about this idea of a Parent–Teacher Association,' I began to Mrs Bonny.

A bright smile lit her face. 'It's a marvellous idea, isn't it?' she said enthusiastically, and I felt my spirits sink. 'All the Caxley schools seem to have them, and the parents are wonderful – always raising money for things, and in and out of the school, helping, you know.' My face must have registered my misgivings, for she gazed at me anxiously. 'You don't think it would work here?' she queried.

There was a pause whilst she darted to the front row and ran an expert finger round the inside of a child's mouth and removed a wet red bead.

'That would *hurt* if you swallowed it,' she said sternly. 'And what's more,' she added practically, 'we're very short of beads.'

She turned to me. 'Sorry, Miss Read. What's your objection to a PTA?'

I told her, somewhat lamely, I felt. It was quite apparent that she was strongly in favour of setting up one, and I could see I was going to be heavily outnumbered.

'I think you would find it a great help,' she assured me. 'I'd welcome it myself.' She stopped suddenly, and her pink face grew pinker. 'But there – I might not be here to enjoy it,' she said, looking confused.

Novelists talk about a cold hand gripping their heroine's heart. Two cold ones gripped mine, and fairly twisted it into oblivion. The thought of losing Mrs Bonny and all that that entailed – the succession of 'supply' teachers, if any, or, much more likely, the squashing of the whole school into my class-room for me to instruct for some dreadful interminable period, froze my blood. It has happened so often before, and every time, it seems, is more appalling than the last.

'Mrs Bonny,' I said, in a voice cracked with apprehension, 'what do you mean?'

She rearranged her pearls self-consciously, slewing them round with energetic jerks to get the clasp tidily at the nape of her neck.

'I was going to tell you on Friday,' said Mrs Bonny. To give me time, I thought despairingly, to recover from the news during the weekend.

'I am getting married again. In the Christmas holidays, in fact.'

I professed myself delighted, and waited for a bolt from heaven to strike me dead.

'A friend of my husband's,' she said, warming to her theme. 'He's always been so close to our family. In fact, he's godfather to my boy.'

'Well, he's jolly lucky,' I said, and meant it, stopping a string of beads which a boy was whirling round and round in a dangerous circle, and getting a bruised hand in the process. The occupational hazards of an infants' teacher are something which would surprise the general public, if explained.

'I don't want to give up teaching, at least for some time. We want to save as much money as we can for when we retire. Anyway, I should miss the children terribly.'

'That's a relief,' I told her.

'We thought we'd see how things go. Theo says that if I find it too much, then I must stop, of course. But I shall stay as long as I can.'

'Let's hope it's for years,' I said.

'So you see,' concluded Mrs Bonny happily, 'although I think the PTA is a marvellous idea – and I think you will too, if it happens, Miss Read – I won't press you one way or the other, because it won't really affect me, will it?'

'No,' I said morosely. 'I quite see that.'

I renewed my congratulations, smiled brightly upon the infants, and returned to my own classroom.

There I found that the children had put away their work, books had been stacked neatly on the cupboard, the large hymn-book had been propped upon the ancient piano in readiness for the next morning's prayers, and all that the class awaited was the word to go home.

Certainly, the clock's hands were at five to four, but I felt slightly nettled at such officious time-keeping. The children, however, arms folded, stout country boots neatly side by side, were so pleased with their efforts that I had not the heart – broken-spirited woman that I was – to chide them.

They sang grace lustily, and then tumbled out into the lobby, while I locked my desk. An ear-splitting shriek, followed by a babble of voices, took me to the lobby in record time.

Mrs Pringle, broom upheld like Britannia's trident, gazed wrathfully upon the horde milling round her.

'If I'm laid up tomorrow,' she boomed, 'lay it at the door of that boy.'

She pointed to Joseph Coggs, whose dark eyes looked piteously towards me.

'Stepped full on me bunion with his great hobnail boots! Enough to cripple me for life!'

I looked at the terrified Joseph.

'Have you said you were sorry?'

'Yes, miss,' he whispered abjectly.

Mrs Pringle snorted. For some unworthy reason my spirits rose unaccountably.

'Ah well, Mrs Pringle,' I said, with as much gravity as I could muster, 'we all have our troubles.'

5. MAKING A START

Trouble was certainly looming for Peter Hale. The two surveys confirmed that there was dry rot in the ground floor of the cottages, and in one king beam, and that rising damp at the back of the property was causing considerable damage to the fabric of the outer walls.

'Nevertheless,' said Mr Croft, the architect, 'there is nothing to worry about. All these little matters can be put right.'

He leant back in his swivel armchair and surveyed Peter Hale benevolently. He was the senior partner in the firm of Croft & Cumberland, and something of a personage in Caxley. He was a man of unusual appearance, affecting from his youth rather long hair and a style of dress which blended the artist with the country gentleman.

His tweed suits were pale, and with them he wore a bow tie which carefully matched them in colour. His shirts were always made of white silk, and he wore a wide-brimmed hat at a jaunty angle. Someone once said that Bellamy Croft was the cleanest man in Caxley, and certainly his face shone with soap and his hair, now white, formed a fluffy halo round his gleaming pink scalp. A whiff of eau-de-Cologne accompanied him, and was particularly evident when he shook out the large vivid silk handkerchiefs he affected.

Caxley's more sober citizens thought Bellamy Croft rather a popinjay, but as time passed he was looked upon as a distinguished member of the community, and the results of his work were much admired.

As a young man, he had spent some years in India when the British Raj held sway. Indian princes had employed him, and he had worked on some projects instigated by Sir Edwin Lutyens himself. Caxley was impressed by this exotic background, but even more impressed with the solid work he did in their own neighbourhood when he settled there.

Now, nearing seventy, he took on only those projects which he liked, and certainly only those within easy range of the Caxley office. The conversion of old property was a speciality of his, and Tyler's Row attracted him.

Peter Hale knew he was lucky to have his services, but was a little apprehensive about the cost of the job.

'I don't want Bellamy Croft to run away with the idea that I'm one of his Indian-prince clients with strong-rooms stuffed with emeralds and rubies of pigeon-egg size, and diamonds too heavy to lift,' he said to Diana. 'Do you think he has any idea of teachers' salaries?'

'Of course he has,' replied Diana robustly. 'Anyway, ask him. If he's outrageously expensive, we'll manage without him.'

'Impossible,' said Peter. 'He knows his stuff, and will see that old Fairbrother gets on with the building properly. I don't grudge Croft's fee – it'll be an investment – but I must see that he doesn't get carried away with all kinds of schemes for improving the place.'

'What do you expect? A miniature Taj Mahal rising between Mrs Fowler's and Sergeant Burnaby's?'

'Not quite, but I intend to keep a tight rein on him. He's already contemplating shutters, and a sort of Chinese porch which would set us back a hundred or two, I can see he'll want watching.'

Now, on this bright August morning, Peter did his best to impress upon Bellamy Croft the absolute necessity of keeping costs as low as possible.

'This dry rot. What will it cost to put right?'

Bellamy told him, and Peter flinched.

'And a damp course?'

'I should prefer to tell you that after I have had a longer look at the place. But we ought to make a good job of it while we're about it. No point in cheese-paring.'

'Naturally. The essentials must be done, and done well.

But I simply haven't the money to indulge in extras such as this porch you show in the plan. Heaven knows what I'll get for my present home – a lot, I sincerely hope, but the bridging loan from the bank must be met eventually, and I'm determined to cut my coat according to the cloth. Maybe we can do all the fancy bits when the other two cottages become vacant.'

'Ah yes, indeed! Stage two,' said Bellamy, shuffling enormous sheets of crackling paper upon the desk. 'I quite appreciate your position – and frankly, I'm glad to work for a man who knows his mind. Stage one, the conversion of the middle two cottages, we can keep very simple, and by the time we've reached stage two we shall know how much more you feel able to embark upon.'

His bland pink face was creased in smiles. He looks happy enough, thought Peter, but then he doesn't have to foot the bill. Was it a hare-brained project he had started? What other snags, besides dry rot, rising damp, two awkward tenants, a jungle of a garden and an architect with alarmingly lavish plans did the future hold?

Was he going to bless or curse the day he decided to buy Tyler's Row?

Time alone would tell.

What with one thing or the other it was well on into August by the time the contract was signed and the die cast.

One sultry afternoon, Diana and Peter drove over to their new property with a formidable collection of gardening tools in the back of the car.

'Do you really think you'll need that enormous great pick axe?'

'It's a mattock,' corrected Peter. 'And the answer's "Yes". It will probably be the most useful tool of the lot. You won't need that trowel and hand fork, you've so hopefully put in, until next season.'

The gate still scraped a deepening semi-circle in the path as they pushed it open.

'I must see to that,' said Peter, shaking his head.

They carried the tools into the back garden and surveyed the jungle with mingled awe and dismay.

'Look at the height of those nettles!' said Diana.

'Take a look at the brambles! Tentacles like octopuses – or do I mean octopi? And those prickles! We really need a flame-thrower before we can begin with orthodox tools.'

He picked up a bill hook and stepped bravely into the weeds, followed by Diana carrying a pair of shears.

'We'll start at the bottom of the garden and work our way towards the house,' Peter said. 'Knock off the top stuff first, and burn it as we go.'

It was hot work. Faraway could be heard the rumblings of a storm, and dark clouds massed ominously on the horizon. Thousands of tiny black thunder-flies settled everywhere, maddening them with their tickling, and swarming into their hair, ears and eyes. Their labours were punctuated by slapping noises as they smote the unprotected parts of their bodies which were under constant attack from the tormentors.

They had been working for about an hour, and had cleared a strip about two yards wide across the width of the garden, when they became conscious of Mrs Fowler watching them sharply over the hedge.

'Oh, good afternoon,' called Diana, wiping her sticky face on the back of her glove. 'As you see, we're just making a start on this terrible mess.'

'There's some good rhubarb just where you're standing,' replied Mrs Fowler austerely. 'And there used to be a row of raspberry canes. Looks as though you've cut them down now.'

Diana refused to be daunted. 'Well, there it is,' she said lightly. 'We shall have to start from scratch, it's obvious. It's impossible to tell weeds from plants now that it's got to this state.'

'Should have been seen to weeks ago,' continued Mrs Fowler. 'All them weeds have seeded and blown over into my garden. Never had so much groundsel and couch grass in my life.'

Peter straightened his back and came to his wife's support.

'And ground elder,' went on Mrs Fowler, before he could say anything, 'and them dratted buttercups. Bindweed, chickweed, docks, the lot! All come over from this parch.'

'Any poison ivy?' asked Peter mildly. 'Or scold's-tongue?'

Mrs Fowler looked suspicious. 'Don't know those, but if there's any over there it'll be in here by now.'

'I'm glad to see you, anyway,' said Peter. 'I was going to knock to tell you we're going to make a bonfire of this lot, in case you had washing hanging out, or wanted to close the windows.'

Mrs Fowler drew in her breath in a menacing manner, but said nothing. She nodded, and retired to her house. A few sharp bangs told the toilers that the windows were being slammed shut.

'What an old bitch she is!' remarked Peter conversationally, slashing at a clump of nettles.

'Peter, don't!' begged Diana. 'She'll hear you.'

'Do her good,' he said, unrepentant. 'Pass the rake, and we'll get the bonfire going before it rains.'

At that moment they heard a loud cough. Sergeant Burnaby's sallow face loomed above the other hedge like a harvest moon.

'Good afternoon sir. Just made a pot of tea, and hope you and the lady will do me the honour of takin' a cup.'

'How kind,' said Diana. 'I'd love one.'

Peter looked less pleased. He was a man who liked to finish the job in hand.

'I want to get the bonfire started before the storm breaks.'

'Let me take the green stuff over the hedge for my fowls,' urged Sergeant Burnaby eagerly. 'They dearly love a bit to pick at, and it'll help you get rid of it.'

'Fine,' said Peter, brightening. He gathered an armful of grass, docks, hogweed and sow thistle and staggered with it to the hedge.

There was a flustered squawking as Sergeant Burnaby flung it over the wire, and then a contented clucking as the hens scattered the largesse with busy legs.

'May as well let them have the lot,' observed their master, after the fourth load had been deposited.

Peter obediently scraped together the last few wisps, and as he did so, a crack of thunder, immediately above, made them jump. A spatter of raindrops fell upon them.

'Come straight in, ma'am,' called Sergeant Burnaby, retreating up the path.

'Run for it!' shouted Peter, snatching the tools together, and within two minutes they were in the old soldier's kitchen, shaking the rain from their clothes.

Everything looked remarkably clean and tidy, thought Diana, when one considered that the lone occupant was approaching eighty.

There was a kitchen range identical with their own in the next cottage, against one wall, but this one was glossy with blacklead, and on the mantelshelf above were several brass ornaments, including a large round clock, all shining.

Among them Diana saw a little embossed box, and following her gaze, the old man took it down for her to handle. It was quite heavy, and bore a medallion showing the head of Princess Mary.

'Sent to us in the Great War,' said the sergeant, with pride. 'We was in the trenches at the time. Christmas present, it was, filled with tobacco. We all thought a lot of that, I can tell you. My old pal, Jim Bennett, he treasured his too. It gets a rub-up every Saturday.'

'I should think that all your lovely things get a rub-up weekly,' said Diana, handing back the box. 'Does anyone come to help you?'

'Not a soul,' said Sergeant Burnaby proudly. 'I don't want no help. That Mrs Fowler come once, early on, but it was only to snoop round. I sent her packing.'

He stirred his cup with a large teaspoon, and looked fierce. 'I'm not one to speak ill,' he continued.

Diana waited for him to do just that, and was not disappointed.

'But that old besom needs watching, sir. Tongue like a whip-lash, and not above nicking anything that's going. Why, the moment the Coggses and Waitses left, she was in them gardens diggin' up what she fancied! They come back, a week after they'd moved, to dig up a row of potatoes, but they was gone. "Next door," I told 'em! "You have to look in the shed next door. You'll find 'em all right. Sacked up for the winter!"' He sniffed at the remembrance. 'Them Waitses never done nothing about it. Too easy-going by half. Always was. But good neighbours to me. I miss 'em.'

Diana exchanged a glance with her husband. Peter's face bore the impatient look of a schoolmaster suffering tale-telling, and about to take retaliatory action.

'Your flowers are so pretty,' said Diana hastily, rising to look out of the window.

The rain drummed down relentlessly, spinning silver coins on the flagstones and the seat of the wooden armchair outside the back door. The bright patch of marigolds, cornflowers and shirley poppies, was a blur through the streaming window, but Diana's comment had succeeded in stemming the old man's venom and in soothing her husband's irritation.

'I like a bit of colour,' said Sergeant Burnaby. 'I dig over a bit near the house and fling in packets of seeds – annuals, you know, all higgledy-piggledy. Don't take a minute, and there's a fine bright sight for the summer.'

He turned to Peter.

'You plannin' to do anything about the thatch?' he asked.

Peter looked cautious. 'Not at the moment,' he replied. 'The architect is still studying things.'

He did not care to tell the sergeant that the thatch would probably be renewed, or at least repaired in stage two, after the demise of his host.

'The window frames are rotten,' continued the sergeant. 'And my chimney don't look too healthy.'

'They'll be seen to,' said Peter, more frankly. These things were included in stage one, he seemed to remember. 'Can't do it all at once, you know, but we'll put things ship-shape as soon as we can.'

'You see,' said Sergeant Burnaby, filling Peter's cup again before he could refuse, 'my end of this row gets all the weather. You'll find that's true, sir. Now, old Mrs Vinegar-Bottle up the other end, she'll worry the guts out of you – pardon me, ma'am – about what wants doin', but her place is a king to this.

47

Sheltered, see, from the westerlies. And her old man kept things up together, so I'm told, when he was alive.'

He spooned sugar briskly from a glass bowl into his cup. 'One, two, three, four,' he counted under his breath.

Diana suppressed a shudder. It must taste like thin golden syrup.

'Poor devil!' commented the sergeant. 'He's better off, wherever he is. That old cat must have helped him to the grave, I don't doubt.'

Peter drained his cup, and stood up. 'Time we were off. Very kind of you to give us tea.'

'Very kind,' echoed Diana.

The old man looked suddenly old and pathetic. 'Must you go? Don't see much company, you know. No need to hurry away on my account. I've got some old photos of this place you might like to see.'

He began to open the table drawer, in a flustered way.

Diana's heart smote her. 'We'd love to, some other time. We really must go now, and pack up our tools.'

'But it's still raining,' protested the old man, trying in vain to keep his guests.

'Can't be helped,' said Peter firmly. 'We'll have another go at the garden as soon as we can. And there's plenty of marking waiting for me at home too which I must go and tackle.'

He held out his hand, and smiled at Sergeant Burnaby.

'I know you'll forgive us for hurrying away,' he said with sudden gentleness. 'But you'll be seeing quite a lot of us in the next few weeks. Too much probably.'

They escaped into the pouring rain, collected their things, and drove home through the storm to Caxley.

The Hales spent the grey, wet evening in their armchairs. Diana's hands were busy with knitting a pale blue coat for a god-daughter's baby. Her head was busy with thoughts of their two tenants.

What on earth had they taken on?

Peter's thoughts were engaged with his history marking. His red pen ticked and slashed its way across the pages. Every now and again he gave a snort of impatience.

'Sometimes I wonder if Lower Fourths can take in American history,' he said, slapping shut one grubby exercise book. 'Young Fellowes here informs me that the Northern Abortionists – a phrase used five times – were extremely active in the nineteenth century.'

'Northern Abortionists?' echoed Diana, bewildered.

'"Abolitionists" to everyone else in the form,' explained Peter, reaching for his pipe. 'But not to young Fellowes, evidently. He's the sort of boy who writes the first word that enters his head. It might just as well have been the Northern Aborigines, or Abyssinians, or anything else beginning with Ab.'

He patted the books into a neat pile.

'That'll do for tonight,' he said firmly. 'They don't have to be returned until term starts.'

'Only another fortnight,' said Diana, 'and so little done at Tyler's Row.'

'What's the hurry? Look upon it as a hobby. It's no good fretting about delay, and we're in the hands of Bellamy and the builder anyway.'

'But nothing seems to be happening.'

'It will soon enough,' Peter assured her.

He spoke more truly than he knew.

6. THE PROBLEM OF TYLER'S ROW

Work began at Tyler's Row towards the end of September, and Diana and Peter grew quite excited when they saw how much had been accomplished after ten days. Everything movable, the old kitchen range, the light fittings, the worm-eaten dresser – even some of the wallpaper – had gone, and the two cottages appeared to be stripped for action.

What they failed to realize in their innocence, was the fact that the first stages of any building work are rapid and quickly apparent. It is the last stages which are so maddeningly prolonged, when plasterers wait for plumbers, and plumbers wait for electricians, and decorators wait for the right paint and wallpaper, and the owners wait to get into the place, with the growing conviction that the mad-house will claim them first.

Those despairing days were still in the future, but already things were becoming complicated for the Hales in the early part of the term. The headmaster, knowing that Peter was intending to move, asked if he might buy his present house.

'My son John comes back from Singapore before Christmas. They've three children now, and another on the way, and your house would be ideal.'

'We shan't be out of it until well after Christmas,' said Peter.

'Surely a couple of cottages won't take all that time to put to rights?'

'They're doing pretty well at the moment,' replied Peter, 'but Bellamy Croft won't be hurried, and I think John will have to look elsewhere if he wants to bring the family straight into a house.'

'He might get temporary accommodation,' mused the headmaster aloud. 'Until you're ready, I mean.'

And a very pleasant situation that would be, thought Peter, with a harassed family man breathing down his neck, urging him into a half-finished Tyler's Row. He was not going to be hustled into anything, he told himself sturdily.

But this was only the beginning. It was amazing how many people decided that Peter Hale's house was exactly what they, or their relations, had been waiting for, and he found himself accosted in Caxley High Street on several occasions by would-be buyers. He had two stock answers. The house was not on the market yet, and wouldn't be until Tyler's Row was ready. Masters & Jones would be the people to approach. He was not handling it himself.

It was all a trifle wearing, although it was some comfort to know that it looked as though the house would sell easily.

And then there was the architect. Peter had said that Bellamy Croft would not be hurried. He was beginning to wonder if he went to Tyler's Row at all. There were several things he wanted to talk to him about, but he never seemed to be in the office, and his secretary was a past-master in covering up for him. Always, it appeared, Bellamy was at work in some remote village, or had gone to consult someone at Oxford or London or Cheltenham.

'I'll ask him to ring you,' was the nearest Peter ever got to seeing the elusive fellow, but he waited in vain for the telephone to ring. And when, after several frustrating weeks it did, Bellamy's apologies were so profuse and disarming that Peter's ire evaporated.

However, it was soon revived by discovering that Bellamy had returned to his fight for a mock-Gothic porch in the centre of Tyler's Row.

'I'm not having it!' he told Diana firmly. 'I'm not being saddled with a Chinese-Chippendale porch, with a pointed lead roof, costing about two hundred smackers, when I want a simple affair with a thatch on top!'

'You did ask him to do the job!' pointed out Diana.

'If I asked the butcher for two pork chops,' replied Peter heatedly, 'I'm damned if I'd accept a saddle of mutton just because he wanted me to have it. My God, what a battle it all is!'

As term progressed, the outlook grew steadily gloomier. Peter began to get headaches – a most unusual thing for so healthy a man.

'Nothing that exercise won't cure,' he insisted, setting out on a four-mile walk whenever he was so afflicted.

'Perhaps you need new reading glasses,' suggested Diana solicitously.

'No, no. These are perfectly adequate. A spell in the fresh air and plenty of muscle-work's the answer.'

And he would vanish for an hour or so, and return rather more exhausted than when he set out; certainly in no mood to tackle the piles of marking which always stand about a school-master's sitting-room.

It was at this stage that Diana found their roles reversed. She, who had been so full of doubts about the move, now did the comforting.

'It will sort itself out. There are bound to be set-backs. All progress goes in fits and starts – two steps forward, and one back – and if you think of Tyler's Row a couple of months ago, and then today, it's really quite heartening.'

Peter refused to be consoled. 'The time they take!' he stormed, raising fists to heaven. 'You'd think three men plus an architect would get the place done in a month! When I think that this is only *stage one* of Bellamy's plan, I wonder if I'll ever live to see stage two. Or even if I *want* stage two, or will be able to raise the money for it. As far as I can see, we'll be looking for a nice little Eventide Home for the Aged by the time stage one's done.'

Autumn gales, of unprecedented ferocity, ripped away tarpaulins fixed over empty window frames and created more work at Tyler's Row. Copper piping and bathroom fittings, left overnight in the empty cottage, disappeared in the small hours and had to be replaced, with infuriating difficulty. Mr Roberts' cows, in a field adjoining the property, pushed their way into the garden and helped themselves to the freshly-planted per-ennials which Diana had spent three afternoons arranging carefully in a newly-dug border. The garden was pock-marked with large holes where they had browsed undisturbed for hours.

At one point, Bellamy Croft, in an expansive mood, had said that there was a possibility of moving in by Christmas. In January he said, somewhat more cautiously, that it might be possible at the end of the month.

In February he said what a trying winter it had been for builders ('And for schoolmasters!' Peter had snarled), and he was truly surprised to find how much there still needed to be done. Perhaps, in early March . . . ?

In the middle of that month, with the end of term in sight, Peter issued an ultimatum.

'We're moving during the Easter holidays, come hell or high-water,' he told Bellamy. 'My own house is sold, and the chap wants to move in. Put some dynamite behind old Fair-brother and his minions, or they'll find themselves having to work round us. They've got three weeks to finish.'

Bellamy Croft professed himself pained and astonished at such impatience, though, in truth, he met with it often enough with his clients. However, Peter's forbidding detention-for-you-boy look had some effect, and a slightly brisker pace of progress began at Tyler's Row.

Although there were cupboards still to be fitted, some top-coat painting to be done and the lavatory window was still missing, Peter and Diana pressed on with their preparations for the move, and named the day as the twentieth of April.

'The relief,' sighed Diana, 'at having something settled at last! Who was it kept saying his patience was exhausted, Peter?'

'Hitler.'

'Are you sure?' Diana sounded startled.

'Positive. His patience was exhausted just before he snapped up yet another country.'

'Well, I never expected to ally myself with that man, but at the moment I can sympathize with his feelings.'

*

Fairacre, of course, had watched the progress of conversion with unabated interest. The theft of the copper piping was attributed at once to Arthur Coggs, although no one had a shred of evidence to prove the charge. It was noted, however, that Mrs Coggs was unusually free with her money at the Christmas jumble sale, even going so far as to expend a shilling on a fur tippet, once the property of Mrs Partridge's mother. This, said some, proved that there was more money than usual in the Coggs' household and where had it come from? Funny, wasn't it, they said, that the copper piping had vanished only a few days earlier?

Others pointed out that any proceeds from the sale of the stolen goods would have been poured promptly down Arthur Coggs' throat in The Beetle and Wedge. Mrs Coggs would have been the last person to receive any bounty from her husband.

Sergeant Burnaby enjoyed every minute of the builders' company, sitting in his old armchair in the garden and carrying on a non-stop conversation with anyone available. He had never had so much excitement and company before. Every day brought another enthralling episode in this living serial story, and he delighted in regaling Peter and Diana with a blow-by-blow account of all that went on between their visits.

Mrs Fowler, on the other hand, behaved with mouth-pursed decorum. She knew, however, quite as much about the doings next door as did Sergeant Burnaby, and kept a watch upon the workmen as vigilant as his, but more discreet.

The schoolchildren were equally interested, shouting to the builders as they passed on the way to school, begging for pieces of putty, nails, strips of wood, pieces of wallpaper, broken tiles and anything else to be treasured.

Mrs Pringle and I were in rare unity in trying to discourage them from pillaging in this way, and from bringing their loot into the school. Well-worked putty leaves finger-prints on exercise and reading books, and the children's fingers were grubbier than ever with handling their newly-found possessions.

I tried to convey to them the fact that they were stealing, with small success.

'But they was going to be thrown out,' they told me. 'Them workmen said as these bits was rubbish.'

'And the putty?' I would persist remorselessly.

'Jest an odd bit, miss,' they would plead.

'Who do you think pays for the putty?'

'Don't know, miss.'

'Mr and Mrs Hale are paying for it. You are just as bad as the thief who took their copper piping.'

'But the workmen –'

'The workmen have no business to give the things away.'

I made little headway with my arguments. The magpie instinct in children is strong, and they could see endless possibilities in the odds and ends so easily obtained. I have always kept a large box in the classroom filled with such oddments as cotton-reels, matchboxes, odd buttons, scraps of material, lino, off-cuts of wood, corks and so on, in which the children love to rummage. From this flotsam and jetsam of everyday life they produce dozens of playthings for themselves, and prize them more than any 'boughten' toy, as they say.

One bleak January morning, after prayers had been said and the register marked, there came a crash from the lobby and a loud wail.

On investigation, I found Joseph Coggs surveying the fragments of a tile scattered over the brick floor of the cloakroom. His dark eyes were shining with tears.

'And what,' I said sternly, 'makes you so late?'

'I bin to get this for my mum.' He pointed a filthy finger towards the pieces.

'From Tyler's Row?'

'Yes, miss. It's going to be –' He sniffed, and corrected

himself. 'It *were* going to be a teapot stand. For her birthday, miss. Saturday, miss.'

'I shouldn't think your mother would want a stolen teapot stand,' I said, improving the shining hour.

'She wouldn't know,' explained Joseph patiently.

Despair began to grip me. Should I ever succeed in my battle?

'You are late. You have been pilfering, despite all I've said, and you've made a mess on Mrs Pringle's clean floor. Sweep it up, and come inside the minute you've finished.'

'Yes, miss,' said Joseph meekly, setting off for the dustpan and brush.

He was disconsolate for the rest of the morning. I could see that he was grieving for his lost treasure, and when he refused second helpings of school dinner – minced beef and mashed potato followed by treacle pudding – my hard heart was softened a little.

When they went out to play, in a biting east wind, I

returned to the school house across the playground, and sorted out a number of objects to add to the contents of the rubbish box.

'You are free to choose,' I told the children when Handiwork lesson began that afternoon. 'You can paint a picture, or get on with your knitting, or make something from the rubbish box.'

Half a dozen little girls drew out their garter-stitch scarves and composed themselves happily with their knitting needles. About the same number of both sexes made for the paints and brushes, but the larger proportion of non-knitters rushed excitedly to the box. Some had seen me adding material and were agog to have first pick.

As I hoped, Joseph was among them. I watched him remove a piece of lino with one hand, and a large wooden lid, once the stopper of a sugar jar – with the other. His expression was one of mingled hope and anxiety. Which, he seemed to be asking himself, would make a replacement for the broken tile?

He took both objects back to his desk, and studied them closely, stroking them in turn. Around him work began on the construction of dolls' beds, dolls' chests-of-drawers, paper windmills and cardboard spinning tops. There was a hubbub of conversation among the manufacturers, but Joseph remained silent, engrossed in his problem.

At length, he set aside the lino and put the flat circle of wood in front of him. Then he went to the side table which holds such necessary equipment as nails, paste, gummed paper, string and so on. He selected some squares of gummed paper, yellow, green, and red, returned to his desk and cut out a number of bright stars.

For the rest of the lesson he stuck them on the lid in ever-diminishing circles. Despite the finger-prints, the result had a primitive gaiety, and it was good to see the child growing happier as the wood was covered. When the last star was in place, he sat and gazed at it enraptured. Then a thought struck him. He came to my desk.

'Will them stars come off under a teapot?'

'Not if you varnish them,' I told him. He made his way to the side table again without a word, and tipped a little varnish into the old saucer kept for the purpose. When the lesson ended the teapot stand was put on the piano to dry, with all the other objects.

'You've made some nice things,' I told the children. 'Are you pleased with your teapot stand, Joseph?'

'Yes, miss. It's for my mum's birthday, miss. Come Saturday miss.'

'And it's honestly come by,' I said meaningly.

'And all out of bits thrown away,' commented Ernest gleefully.

'Like my tile,' added Joseph.

I opened my mouth, thought better of it, and closed it again.

'There's a fine old mess in my dustpan,' grumbled Mrs Pringle when she arrived after school that afternoon. 'Full of bits of broken tile or something.'

'Joseph should have tipped that in the dustbin,' I said.

Mrs Pringle snorted. 'Been pinching again? Them Coggses is all tarred with the same brush, if you ask me. Tyler's Row, I suppose? Wonder that place isn't gutted by now. Don't know what children are coming to these days. We'd 'ave got a good leathering when I was young, but today – why, the kids don't seem to know right from wrong.'

'It's not for want of telling,' I told her, with feeling.

PART TWO

Some Squally Showers

* * * *

7. MOVING DAY

Providence, kindly for once, sent sunshine on April 20th. Diana had dreaded the day of departure from her old home, but when it arrived, the house looked so strange and bare that she felt as though the parting with it were already over.

Then, too, there was so much to do that there was little time to wax sentimental. Much of the stuff was already at Tyler's Row, for they had been taking over boxes of books, china and cutlery during the last week or so.

They ate their breakfast in the depleted kitchen, with boxes of kitchen utensils stacked around them. The final stages of packing Diana found completely numbing.

'What on earth shall I do with this milk?' she asked, looking hunted, as she held up a jug.

'Chuck it down the sink,' said Peter robustly. 'And throw the rest of the cornflakes and bread to the birds.'

She obeyed, and then stood, looking bewildered. 'Suppose we want a drink later on? I ought to have kept out the flasks, you know, and filled them with coffee.'

'There's a pub at Fairacre, and old Burnaby will be making pots of tea like mad. Don't fret so,' said Peter impatiently.

Diana moved dumbly about her tasks. Most women, she told herself, would have thought about flasks and sandwiches and all the preparations for a move. She felt decidedly inefficient and slightly despairing. What, for instance, did she do with the last wet teacloth?

The removal men were due at nine-thirty. Peter was going ahead to let them into Tyler's Row, and Diana was left behind to see things out. Later, Peter would return to fetch her and Tom the cat, whose basket stood on the kitchen dresser in readiness.

'You must leave Tom's saucer,' said Diana, watching Peter cram the last-minute objects into the laundry basket. 'He likes a drink about eleven.'

'Oh my lord!' moaned Peter, clutching his head. 'Tom'll have to go without today. Anyway we've thrown away the milk.'

'Oh dear! He'll go next door for Charlie's. You know what he is!'

'He won't if you shut him in the bedroom,' replied Peter firmly. 'Now, I'm off. Don't panic. Leave it all to the men, and I'll pick you up as soon as I've seen the furniture settled. Probably soon after one.'

Within minutes of his departure the furniture vans arrived, and from then on four hefty men took over. Diana wandered vaguely from room to room, trying to keep out of their way. They seemed remarkably calm and efficient, with their tea-chests and mounds of newspapers, and pieces of sacking and polythene sheeting.

She watched the largest of the four deftly wrapping her best tea-set in pieces of newspaper, his great red hands handling each piece much more delicately than she could herself.

There was something very sad about uprooting all these things – worse, in a way, than uprooting oneself. A box of oddments, left for the daily woman, seemed particularly pathetic to Diana. There was the blue and white mixing bowl which Mrs Jones had always admired, and over there, waiting to be packed, was the blue and white flour dredger which had always stood beside it. It seemed wrong that they should be parted after so many years. Somehow, Diana was reminded of a family dispersed, a bond broken, each wrenched from a common home, and scattered afar.

By mid-morning the upstairs floor was stripped, and Diana's roving feet echoed dismally on the bare boards. In the spare bedroom, a disgusted cat lashed his tail and did his best to escape as the door opened. He was as upset as Diana by this outrageous shattering of routine. No after-breakfast stroll in the garden, no visiting of Charlie, the next-door Siamese, to polish off his breakfast, no mid-morning snack – it was enough to put a cat in a rage, and Tom indulged his fury to the utmost. He repelled Diana's sympathetic advances, wriggling from her arms, and gazing at her malevolently from the window sill. He had noticed the hated cat basket earlier in the day, and knew that something unpleasant was afoot. Another trip to see the vet? Another stay at the kennels? Whatever was planned was not going to be approved by Tom, and he showed his displeasure plainly.

Diana left him to his sulking, and went from bedroom to bedroom to make sure that nothing had been overlooked. The rooms, without the curtains, were amazingly light, and the walls seemed remarkably dirty. There were grubby lines where the chests of drawers and chair had stood. There was even a patch on the wall above Peter's bed, where his head must have rested when he read at night. Diana had never noticed it before, and thought the rooms looked startlingly seedy without their furnishings.

The oddest things seemed to have come to light. Whose was this grey hairpin by the skirting board? She had never used a hairpin in her life, and certainly not a grey one. In the boys' old room, a china bead and the bayonet broken from a lead soldier glinted in the crack of the floorboards. A papery butterfly clung to their window, and in a dark corner were a few minute shreds of paper which looked suspiciously like the work of a mouse.

It was a good thing that Mrs Jones was going to scrub the

place from top to bottom, thought Diana, or the new owners would think that they had lived in absolute squalor. No one, looking at the bare rooms now, would believe that they were thoroughly spring-cleaned each March, and zealously turned out once a week.

By midday the vans were packed, and they rumbled away down the drive. Automatically, Diana looked at the empty mantel shelf to see the time, and even wandered into the kitchen to consult the non-existent wall clock there. Her neighbour had invited her to lunch, and she made her way next door, glad to leave the uncanny silence of her own home.

'How's it going?' asked her hostess.

'Very well, I think. But I feel as though I've been put through a wringer.'

'What you need is a meal,' said her neighbour practically, leading the way.

Over at Tyler's Row the day grew more hectic as it advanced. Peter knew exactly how he wanted the unloading done, and had given explicit directions about labelling the tea-chests so that they could be taken to the right room without any delay.

'Carpets down first,' he had told Diana. 'Then cover them where the men will be treading, and simply put each piece of furniture in place as it's unpacked. It shouldn't take much more than an hour.'

Of course, it did not work out like that. The men had packed the vans with pieces which fitted well together, irrespective of the rooms for which they were intended. A little desultory labelling had been done in the early stages, but most of the tea-chests bore no labels at all. Poor methodical Peter felt his blood pressure rising as the boxes came into the tiny hall, one after the other, with the cheerful cry: 'Where do you want this, sir?'

Diana's camphor-wood blanket chest, brought back from China by a long-dead seafarer in the family, proved to be too

large to go upstairs to the landing which was to have been its resting place.

'But it *must* go up,' said Peter distractedly, watching the men twist it and turn it. The stair wall and the banisters were escaping damage by a hair's breadth. 'I *measured* the thing.'

'But did you measure these 'ere stairs?' puffed one man.

'Of course I did,' snapped Peter.

'Measurements don't help,' said the second man lugubriously. 'When you comes to it, there's always summat as sticks out. Legs, maybe, or an 'andle – or the staircase bulges. I've seen it 'appen time and time again.'

'We could take it through the bedroom window,' suggested the other, 'if we could get it out of the frame.'

'And what about the bedroom door?' cried Peter. 'That's about half the width of the window. No, no. It will have to stay downstairs for the time being.'

'In the 'all?'

'A fat lot of good that would be,' said Peter, sorely tried. 'We can't move as it is for all these unlabelled boxes. Take the thing into the garden shed for now. At least it's out of the way.'

Despite his meticulous work with pencil and paper in the preceding weeks, there were other things besides the blanket chest which Peter found to be too large or too wide for the places appointed. The kitchen door opened on to the cooker. The saucepan shelf proved to be just the right height for the handles to jut out into passers' eyes. The hall floor was so uneven that the grandfather clock leant drunkenly this way and that and they were obliged to put it into the drawing room, displacing a bookcase which eventually joined the blanket chest in the limbo of the garden shed.

But the final straw came when an underfelt was discovered in the van and proved to be the one which should have been put down under the main bedroom carpet, upon which all the heavy furniture was now in position.

The day had been punctuated by visits from Sergeant Burnaby, loving every minute, who offered cups of tea, coffee and general advice non-stop. At four o'clock, exhausted by his tribulations, Peter reeled next door and partook of a cup of well-stewed tea sweetened with condensed milk, which he drank standing, saying, truly, that if he sat down he felt he would never rise again.

At five o'clock the men departed, cheerful to the last, and Peter set off to fetch Diana and Tom.

'I feel about a hundred,' he thought as he drove through Beech Green, dodging a pheasant bent on suicide. 'Talk about preparing for retirement! I doubt if I'll live to see it at this rate.'

And then his spirits rose. They were actually at Tyler's Row! After all the vicissitudes, it was theirs at last! In a few minutes, he and Diana would be driving away from their old home for the last time.

He stepped on the accelerator and sped towards Caxley.

But he had reckoned without Tom, Diana greeted him in some agitation.

'I went to get Tom a few minutes ago, and I swear the door wasn't open wider than three inches! He shot out through the back door, and he must be about six gardens away. I've called till I'm hoarse. What shall we do?'

'Tell Kitty next door. He's bound to turn up tonight for his food, or for Charlie's. We'll come over last thing to collect him, or tomorrow morning.'

Diana departed, and Peter took a look at the empty house. He could understand Diana being upset about the move, he realized suddenly. Such a lot had happened here. Almost all their married life had been spent under this roof. The house had served them well. He hoped the newcomers would be as happy in it.

Diana returned much relieved.

'Kitty will look out for him. It's a pity we're not on the phone yet at Tyler's Row, but she says we're not to dream of turning out again tonight after such a day. She'll keep him in her house overnight.'

They walked slowly down the familiar gravel path.

'Trust Tom,' said Peter, smiling. 'I thought this would be our final exit, but what's the betting we are back and forth like yoyos fetching that damn cat?'

'How's the house?' said Diana.

'A shambles,' replied her husband happily, 'but I've found the drink and the glasses to celebrate getting in at last. We've made it, my dear!'

Later, when the celebratory drinks were over, Diana became unusually business-like.

'Now, the first thing to do is to hang the curtains. Then we must make up the beds and put in hot bottles.'

'What, in this weather?'

'The sheets have been packed in a suitcase for the last two days. They may be damp.'

'Which suitcase?'

'The red one,' said Diana briskly. 'I put everything we should need for the beds in it. Including the bottles.'

'Well, where is it?'

Diana's confidence wavered. 'Here, somewhere. Upstairs, I should think.'

There was no sign of it upstairs. Downstairs, a pile of boxes, holdalls, cases and bundles yielded no red suitcase. Diana, by now, was reduced to her more normal state of vagueness.

'Did you see it go into the van?'

'No. We brought it over ourselves one day this week.'

'Are you sure?'

'I'm not sure of anything now,' cried Diana hopelessly. 'I swear I'll never move again. It's all too exhausting.'

'Have another drink,' said Peter, watching his wife sink on to the settee between a pile of curtains and a mound of the *National Geographical Magazine*.

'No, I'm tiddly enough as it is.'

She pushed her fingers through her hair distractedly. 'I *know* it's here,' she said firmly. 'Think, Peter. You must have seen it during the day.' She fixed him with a glittering stare.

'You frighten the life out of me,' said her husband, 'looking like the Ancient Mariner.'

He stared back, then put down his glass and left the room. In a moment, he returned carrying the case.

'Under the stairs,' he said triumphantly. 'Come to think of it, I put it there myself. I thought it had dusters and brushes and things in it.'

He looked at it more closely.

'But you said a red case. This is brown.'

'It's maroon or burgundy,' said Diana, snapping it open with relief. 'That means red.'

'The only red I recognize is the colour of a pillar box,' said Peter, following his wife with an armful of bed-linen.

By the time the beds were made and the curtains hung in their bedroom and the sitting room they were too tired to do much more.

'I should like a mixed grill,' said Peter. 'A large one – with plenty of kidney.'

'Well, you won't get it, my love,' replied Diana cheerfully. 'I propose to give you a tin of soup prepared by Messrs Crosse and Blackwell's fair hands. That is, if we can find the tin opener. And we might rise to bread and cheese after that. And if you really want high life, you can top up with a banana, rather squashed.'

'It sounds delightful,' said Peter resignedly. 'Do we get breakfast?'

'With luck,' said Diana. 'We'll have to be up early, by the way, to let in the workmen.'

'Well, let's have this rave-up of a meal now,' suggested Peter. 'I'll go out and lock up the shed, and see everything's to rights.'

Outside, a full moon was rising, glowing orange through the light mist that veiled the downs. The air was as fresh as spring water, and the scent of narcissi came from Mrs Fowler's trim garden next door.

Peter breathed in deeply, savouring the beauty of the night, and relishing the thought of happy years to be spent in Fairacre. He turned to look at Tyler's Row.

Through the curtainless kitchen window he could see Diana at the stove. He hoped she would be as happy as he was about the house. She had been so content in Caxley. It would be terrible if she found Fairacre lonely or uncongenial. He must make sure that she settled here easily. It was a good thing, he told himself, that term did not begin for another week or so. They could get the place straight together, and ease the changeover.

Dimmer lights than their own kitchen one shone from the two cottages at each end. A greenish one at Mrs Fowler's suggested that she was watching television. Sergeant Burnaby's glowed as orange as the moon, behind his buff curtains.

'If only all four were empty!' thought Peter. 'If only we could start stage two!'

If, if . . .

His grandmother used to have some tart remark about 'ifs and buts getting you nowhere', he remembered. Maybe she was right. It was enough, for the moment, to be in Tyler's Row, to sleep under its thatch and to have his first meal – austere though that promised to be – in its kitchen.

With a last look at the exterior of his domain, Peter turned to go indoors.

8. An Exhausting Evening

'They're in then,' said Mr Willet as I crossed the playground to go into school. He was perched on a stepladder tying back the American pillar rose which scrambles over the side of the school, clashing hideously with the brickwork, but delighting us all with its bountiful growth.

'Who are?'

'Them new people. Hales. Schoolmaster up Caxley. Took Tyler's Row.'

Mr Willet's staccato delivery was caused more by rhythmic lunges at a high shoot than by impatience with my stupidity.

'Oh yes! I forgot they were moving in. Yesterday, wasn't it?'

'And a nice day they had for it, too,' said Mr Willet, coming down the ladder. 'Very lucky, they was. Not all plain sailing though, from what I hear. Them removable men was a bit slap-handed, and they found the underfelt after they'd put everything in the bedroom.'

'Good lord!'

'You might well say so. Then their blessed cat run off in Caxley and they're having to fetch it today.'

I began to wonder how Mr Willet knew all this. As if he guessed my thoughts, he spoke deprecatingly.

'Not that I know much about it, of course. I'm not one to meddle in other folk's affairs, but you can't help over-hearing things in a village.'

'So I've noticed,' I said, one hand on the school's door handle.

Mr Willet pointed roofwards. 'Couple of sparrows making a nest up the end there. I suppose I dursen't pull it out?'

'No, indeed,' I said firmly. 'I like sparrows.'

'Not many does,' commented Mr Willet.

'I know. I can't think why. I once knew a kind, good-hearted man, very much respected everywhere, who used to catch sparrows and pull off their heads. Quite unlike him really.'

'Very sensible he sounds,' said Mr Willet approvingly. 'They're pestses, is sparrows. Worse'n rats, I reckon.'

'That's as maybe,' I replied, using one of Mrs Pringle's favourite phrases, 'but you can leave that nest alone.'

My caretaker beamed indulgently, and I left the bright sunshine to enter Fairacre School, knowing that the sparrows would be spared.

Later that morning, I decided it was too splendidly sunny to stay indoors, and bade the children dress and accompany me on a saunter round the village. The invitation was received with rapture.

These occasional sorties are officially known as 'nature walks', and to make these outings seem more legitimate we collect such things as twigs, flowers, mosses, feathers, snail shells and other natural objects to take back to the classroom for study.

Naturally, other objects, far more attractive to the children, have to be discarded. Cigarette cartons, bottle tops, nuts and bolts, crisp bags, lengths of wire, tubing, binder twine, broken plastic cups, pieces of glass from smashed windscreens and rear-lights and a hundred other manifestations of civilization are collected, only to be thrown into the school dustbin, amidst general regret.

This morning, the April sunshine was really warm, a pre-view, as it were, of summer days to come. Enormous clouds towered into the blue sky above the downs, moving slowly and majestically in the light breeze. A bevy of larks mounted invisible stairs to heaven, letting fall a cascade of song as they climbed. Cats and dogs sunned themselves on cottage door-steps, and here and there a budgerigar had been hung outside in its cage to enjoy the early warmth and fresh air.

A red tractor, bright as a ladybird, crawled slowly up and down Mr Roberts' large field behind the school, and the children waved energetically to the driver.

'My dad,' said Patrick proudly.

'My uncle,' said Ernest, at the same moment. They were both right. And that, I thought, sniffing at an early white violet, is the best of a village school. It remains, even now, a family affair.

We took the rough lane that leads uphill to the bare downs. For the first hundred yards or so, a few trees and bushes line the path. The thorny sloe trees were already pricked with white blossom, and the black ash buds were beginning to break into leaf along the pewter-grey stems.

Joseph Coggs knelt suddenly down in a patch of dry grass by the side of the lane. 'Got a nail in me shoe,' he explained.

'Us all 'ave,' retorted Patrick, convulsed by his own wit.

Eileen gave a sudden shriek. 'There's a snake, miss! Look, by Jo!'

Sure enough, the last few inches of a small grass snake could be seen slithering for cover among the bushes. Obviously, it had been sunning itself in the grass and was disturbed by Joseph.

'Kill 'un!' shouted some of the boys, advancing with sticks upraised.

'No, it's cruel!' shrieked the girls.

'Leave it alone,' I said firmly. 'It doesn't do any harm. In fact, it does quite a lot of good.'

'That's right,' agreed Ernest, siding with me. 'Grass snakes eat beetles, and frogs, and tadpoles, and earwigs, and worms, and spiders, and slugs, and maggots, and snails and . . .'

He paused for breath.

'Brembutter?' asked someone sarcastically. 'Old knowall!'

This shaft of wit caused more general hilarity. The boys smote each other with juvenile joy. The girls tittered behind their hands, and the snake made good his escape in the general furore.

'See who can get to the top first,' I said suddenly, and watched them stampede uphill, screaming with excitement. I followed at a more sedate pace, relishing my temporary solitude and mentally congratulating the sparrows and the grass snake on their escape from their male predators.

The children's spirits were still high when we returned to the schoolroom, but mine had suddenly plummeted. This very evening the first meeting of the Parent–Teacher Association of Fairacre School was to be held.

My struggles against the formation of this association had been prolonged but necessarily half-hearted. If popular demand clamoured for such a thing, then a headmistress must bend, particularly if she wished to live in amity with her neighbours.

It had been decided by half the committee to make the first meeting a purely social occasion, but the other half had felt that something more earnest and meaty should mark the event. Mrs Johnson and Mrs Mawne were both of this faction.

'I happen to know the president of the Caxley PTA

group,' Mrs Johnson said, with some pride. 'I'm sure I could persuade her to come and give a talk about the aims of the movement.'

After some discussion, a compromise was arranged. Mrs Jollifant would be invited to give a *short* talk, 'a *really brief* talk,' emphasized the vicar, our chairman, 'say, of about fifteen to twenty minutes in length.' This, we all felt, need not take too much time from the main activities of the evening, which would be eating, drinking, listening to a duet played on the school piano by Ernest's mother and aunt, 'Three Little Maids from School' sung by three of the younger mothers, and looking at slides of Mrs Mawne's holiday in Venice, that is if we could find the right plug for the projector. Mrs Johnson had offered to prepare a quiz ('Make it *simple*,' begged the vicar), and would supply pencils and paper for this excitement.

'Now leave your desks tidy,' I exhorted my flock at the end of their school day. 'Your parents may want to look at your books, and they don't want to see half-sucked sweets and lumps of putty, any more than I do.'

There was a feverish scrabbling among their possessions, and the waste-paper basket overflowed in record time. I saw them out thankfully, did my own tidying, and went across to the school house to have an hour or two's breather before facing the rigours of a social evening.

At seven-fifteen, clad in my best black frock which Fairacre knows only too well, I went back to the school room bearing a handsome bowl of King Alfred daffodils which I was lending for the occasion.

It looked rather splendid, I thought, on top of the ancient piano. Mrs Johnson, rushing in two minutes' later, stopped short in her tracks and threw up her hands.

'Well, that thing can't stay there,' she said, advancing upon my beauties. 'The window sill, I think.'

'It's not wide enough,' I said mildly. 'Anyway, what's

wrong with the top of the piano? They show up rather well there.'

'The piano,' explained Mrs Johnson, with ill-concealed impatience, 'is to be *in use*. It will have to be *open* for the duets and the accompaniments.'

'You'll be lucky,' I told her. 'It's never been opened since the skylight dripped on it and the wood swelled.'

Mrs Johnson breathed heavily and turned a little pink, but banged the bowl back on the piano top, and turned away.

Parents began to arrive thick and fast, and I kept a sharp look-out for my old friend Amy, whilst welcoming them at the door. Amy is not a parent at all, but she was at college with me and sometimes does a little 'supply' teaching to keep her hand in. At this time she was helping at the same Caxley school at which our speaker, Mrs Jollifant, was a member of staff. Consequently, Amy had double entry, as it were, into tonight's festivities.

I saw her soon enough, in an exquisitely cut burgundy-red wool frock. One large cabuchon garnet swung on a long gold chain about her neck, and her dark red shoes I mentally priced at twelve pounds. We kissed each other with real affection. Amy, though she tries to boss me, is very dear to me, and the memory of horrors shared at college binds us very close.

'Put me somewhere at the back,' she said, with unusual modesty.

'Not in that frock,' I said. 'You'll sit in the front and delight all eyes.'

The vicar settled matters by taking her arm and leading her to a seat next to his own, and very soon afterwards he opened the proceedings with an admirably clear explanation of the reasons for our being gathered together.

'We are particularly fortunate in having Mrs Jollifant for our speaker,' he said. 'She will be with us in a few minutes, but has to attend another meeting in Caxley first. Meanwhile, we will have a short session of community singing, if someone will give out the booklets.'

I rose to oblige. These dog-eared pamphlets date back to the days of war – the last war, I hasten to add – though you might not think so on reading the contents.

'Pack Up Your Troubles In Your Old Kit-bag' and 'Tipperary' are there, relics of World War One, and 'Goodbye, Dolly, I Must Leave You' carries us right back to the Boer War seventy-odd years ago. However, 'Roll Out The Barrel' redresses the balance a little, and 'She'll Be Coming Round the Mountain' seems positively up-to-date.

At any rate, all Fairacre knows them well, and we sang lustily, to Mrs Moffat's somewhat erratic accompaniment on the piano. The daffodils nodded vigorously on the tightly-closed lid, much to my satisfaction.

When we were exhausted, the vicar introduced Mr Johnson as our next contributor to the general gaiety.

'He is going to sing to us,' said the vicar, with a hint of resignation in his tone which I thought misplaced.

Mr Johnson, clutching a sheet of music, made signals to Mrs Moffat. What would it be? I half-hoped for a spirited rendering of 'The Red Flag'. His three ebullient children had taught the rest of the school a lively ditty in the playground which had become very popular.

It went:

> Let him go or let him tarry,
> Let him sink or let him swim,
> He doesn't care for me
> And I don't care for him:
> For I'm the worker, he's the boss
> And the boss's day is done,
> But the worker's day is coming
> Like the rising of the sun.

But Mr Johnson did no more than sing 'Bless This House' in a pleasant baritone, and with the mildest of expression. I felt cheated, but the general applause was warm.

Mrs Jollifant arrived at this juncture, a dazzling figure in a trouser-suit of shimmering metallic thread. There were some looks of disapproval from the older ladies in the audience, but the young mothers gazed in open admiration.

Her hair was piled high in a tea-cosy style, and was of that intense uniform blackness which only a hairdresser can achieve. She carried a beaded and fringed handbag and an ominously large bundle of notes.

After polite clapping, Mrs Jollifant began her little talk. The time was eight o'clock.

At twenty past, she had covered what she described as 'The preliminary steps to forming a Parent–Teacher Association'. By eight-thirty we had heard of the Necessity For Co-operation,

Keeping Abreast of Modern Methods, and the Need for Constant Discussion Between Parent and Teacher.

The two tea-ladies here tip-toed out across the creaking floorboards to turn down the boiler which was bubbling in readiness for the tea and coffee. I noticed that they did not return.

By ten to nine, a certain amount of fidgeting began, and one or two young mothers whispered agitatedly to each other. Mrs Jollifant's address flowed on remorselessly. Amy, sitting between the vicar and me, sighed noisily, and crossed one elegant leg over the other. I admired the beautiful shoes without envy, and hoped that the rumbling of my stomach was not heard by anyone but myself. A cup of coffee would have been welcome half an hour ago. Now it was needed as a desperate restorative.

St Patrick's church clock struck nine, but this did not perturb our speaker. We had now reached The Benefits to Our Children stage, with a lot of stuff about Flowering Minds, Spiritual Needs and the Sharing of Love and Experience. Every profession, I thought wearily, has its own appalling jargon, but surely Education takes the biscuit.

At nine-fifteen Mrs Mawne rose, with considerable clattering, and said she really must go, as it was getting *so late*. Mrs Mawne does not lack moral courage, and though the general feeling was, no doubt, of disapproval at such behaviour, there was a certain amount of envy as we watched her depart into the night.

The two tea-ladies, emboldened by Mrs Mawne's gesture, now put their heads round the door and asked if they should make the tea.

Mrs Jollifant, not a whit abashed, said she would be exactly five minutes, was exactly fifteen, and at length sat down to thunderous applause activated by relief rather than rapture.

Stiffly, with creaking joints, rumbling stomachs and slight headaches, we made an ugly rush upon the tea, coffee and sandwiches, before embarking on a shortened second half of our social evening.

Later by my fireside, Amy and I caught up with our own affairs. James, her husband, now had to go to London regularly twice a week, and stay overnight, she told me.

'An awful bore for him,' said Amy, fingering her gold chain. 'He brought me back this garnet last week.'

Amy has a collection of beautiful jewellery which James brings home after his business trips. Sometimes I wonder if Amy has suspicions, but she is a loyal wife, and says nothing.

'It's simply lovely,' I said honestly.

'You should wear red,' said Amy, studying me, and looking as though she found the result slightly repellent. 'I've told you before not to wear black. It positively *kills* you.'

'But I've got it! I must wear it. It's hardly been worn at all.'

'Now, that's a flat lie. To my knowledge you've had it four years. You wore it first to my cocktail party.'

'I may have had it four years – that's nothing in Fairacre. I don't get much opportunity to wear this sort of frock. It'll do for another four easily.'

'Put it in the next jumble sale, and buy yourself a red one. Give Fairacre a treat. Or what about a sparkling trouser-suit like Mrs J's?'

'No thanks.'

Amy lit a cigarette.

'Detestable woman! I try and avoid her at school. She wears emeralds with sapphires.'

'Bully for her,' I said. 'I'd like the chance to wear either of 'em. My Aunt Clara's seed pearls are about the nearest I get to the real thing.'

Amy blew three perfect smoke rings in a row, one of the ex-curricular accomplishments I watched her learn at college.

'She's such a phoney,' said Amy. 'All that terrible stuff we heard tonight! If you could only see her three children!'

'No Flowering Minds? No Sharing of Love and Experience?'

'Plenty of that all right,' said Amy darkly. 'The two youngest are at school. The eldest, an unattractive amalgam of hair and spots, is at one of the danker universities in the north. He brought his girl-friend home for the entire vacation. Heavily pregnant too.'

'Is he going to marry her?'

'Well, it's not his baby, so he says, so probably not.'

'What about the other two?'

'Both on probation. One steals, the other fights, and they both lie. I'd give them two years before the mast rather than probation, but of course it does mean Mrs Jollifant gets seen too by the probation officer when he visits.'

'You'd think she'd keep quiet about children,' I said, 'having such horrible children of her own.'

'The Mrs Jollifants of this world,' Amy told me pontifically, 'do not recognize horrible children – least of all their own. By the time your Parent–Teacher Association has brain-washed you, with half-a-dozen speakers like Mrs J, you'll think they're all perfect angels too. Could you squeeze another cup of coffee out of that pot?'

'That'll be the day!' I told her, reaching for the coffee-pot.

9. CALLERS

May, that loveliest of months, surpassed itself as the Hales settled into their new home. Shrubs, which had stood half-hidden by dead grass and weeds when Peter and Diana had first visited Tyler's Row, now flowered abundantly. Lilac bushes, pink, white and deep purple, tossed their scent into the air, and a fine cherry tree dangled its white blossom nearby. Unsuspected bulbs had pushed up bravely, and delighted them with late-flowering narcissi and tulips. Those perennials which had escaped the notice of Mr Roberts' cows, flourished in the fine dark soil, and Diana already made plans for new beds in the autumn.

She was so busy that she had no time to miss the whirl of Caxley's social life. It was a relief, she found, to be free of coffee mornings, bazaars, cheese and wine parties, and all the other fund-raising affairs which she had felt obliged to attend. The invitations still came, but she was able to answer truthfully that she had too much to see to at the moment.

The workmen were still with them, and at times Peter wondered if they would ever go.

'I confidently expect to wrap up Christmas parcels for them,' he commented gloomily, watching their van depart one tea-time. 'I shall give Bert a bottle of shampoo, and Frank a belt to keep up those filthy jeans. Binder twine doesn't appear to do the job.'

Bert and Frank were two cheerful youths, self-styled 'sub-contractors', who were engaged in the last stages of the out-door painting. They were accompanied everywhere by a transistor radio which blared out a stream of pop music to the unspoken despair of Diana, and the very outspoken fury – when he was there to hear it – of Peter. As they plied their brushes, squatting on their haunches or balanced on ladders, they shouted above the din to each other. Diana heard their exchanges and found them incomprehensible.

''E fouled 'im right 'nuff. Ref be blind 'arf the time.'

'Ar! Wants to drop ol' Betts. Never make the fourth round with 'im in goal. See 'im Sat'day?'

Football appeared to be the only topic of conversation, and this was punctuated with occasional bursts of discordant song with transistor accompaniment.

At eleven each morning, Diana made coffee for them. She carried it into the sunshine, and they knocked off with alacrity and sat on the garden seat. Sometimes she sat with them and they told her about their families. To her eyes they appeared only children themselves, but Bert had two boys of his own, and Frank three girls.

After ten minutes, Diana would hurry back to her work, but the two young men remained sitting and smoking until half-past eleven or twenty to twelve.

'Ah well,' one would say, rising reluctantly, 'best get back, I s'pose.'

'Ar! Get the ol' job done,' the other would agree, and they would amble back to their paint brushes, much refreshed.

And their wives, thought Diana, are scrubbing and washing, ironing and cooking and shopping, dressing and undressing young children, and generally running round in circles. And when their husbands get home, no doubt the wives will think indulgently: 'Poor things, they've been working hard all day! Must give them a good meal, and let them have a nice rest while I wash up and put the children to bed!'

Diana's immediate neighbours were not greatly in evidence, she was relieved to find. Certainly, Sergeant Burnaby tended to hover near the dividing hedge whenever she had occasion to go into the garden, and was pathetically eager to prolong any little conversations they had. But her fears that he might make frequent calls proved groundless, and only the rattle of his poker in the grate next door, or the sharp tap-tap caused by knocking out his pipe on the fire-bars, called his presence to mind.

From Mrs Fowler's side, nothing was heard. 'Keeping her-self to herself' was one of her prides, and Diana only had a rare glimpse of her when she hung out some of her dazzling wash-ing, or took a bowl down the garden path to pick some greens.

But if Diana saw little of her neighbour, the same could not be said of Mrs Fowler, who knew nine-tenths of the new-comers' movements. Before a week was out, she knew that the Hales preferred brown bread to white, took one pint of Jersey milk a day, sent sheets, pillowslips, towels – even tea-towels and dusters, which Mrs Fowler thought scandalous – to the laundry, and that Peter Hale used an electric razor, and that the bedside alarm went off at seven o'clock sharp.

Diana was unaware of the intense interest that the village as a whole took in their affairs. She would have been surprised and amused to know that Mr Lamb at the Post Office knew where her two sons were stationed, that the Hales banked with the National Westminster and had monthly accounts with a Caxley garage, butcher and hardware store. He had still to find out who the titled lady was to whom Mrs Hale wrote regularly. (It was, in fact, an elderly aunt.) He was intrigued, too, by the number of letters addressed to a certain Oxford College in Mr Hale's neat hand, but Mr Lamb was used to biding his time, and was confident that all these things would be made clear to him, if he waited long enough.

There had been several callers at Tyler's Row. The vicar, the Reverend Gerald Partridge, and his wife were the first to come, and later Mrs Mawne descended upon Diana when she was engaged in the almost impossible task of pinning up the hem of a frock whilst wearing it. She opened the door to her visitor, very conscious of her uneven hem-line and the half-dozen pins threatening her stockings.

'I know that calling is out of date these days,' said Mrs Mawne when they were seated in the sitting room, 'and a great pity it is, I think. One can feel so lonely in a new place. I know I was quite daunted when I first came to Fairacre. Luckily, my husband had been here for some little time before me, and of course he'd made a number of friends.'

'I thought I would join the Women's Institute,' said Diana. 'It's a very good way of meeting people.'

'*Excellent!*' agreed Mrs Mawne, with energy. 'We can always do with new members, especially on the committee.'

'Well, I don't know –' began Diana, somewhat taken aback.

'Your leg,' said Mrs Mawne, peering through her glasses, 'appears to be bleeding.'

'Confound these pins!' exclaimed Diana, leaping to her feet, and explained her predicament.

'Well, we'll soon put that right,' said Mrs Mawne, and fell upon her knees on the new carpet. 'Hand me the pins and a ruler.'

'They're upstairs,' said Diana. 'One moment, and I'll fetch them.'

For the next five minutes the ladies were engrossed in their task, and Diana thought that Mrs Mawne, formidable though her manner was, certainly had her practical side.

'Now stand still while I crawl round,' said her visitor. She thumped down the school ruler on its end, by one side seam.

'Seventeen,' puffed Mrs Mawne, circumnavigating her hostess, and pausing at intervals with the ruler.

'Seventeen, seventeen, seventeen-and-a-quarter – blast-it! Hold hard a minute!'

After a short battle with the pins, Mrs Mawne professed herself satisfied, and scrambled with difficulty to her feet.

'It's terribly kind of you,' said Diana. 'You couldn't have called at a better time for me. Now let me brush your skirt. This new carpet is shedding whiskers madly.'

Mrs Mawne gave the skirt a perfunctory bang with a massive hand.

'Don't vacuum clean it too much just yet,' she advised. 'Hand brush for a few weeks, I always say, until it's settled in.'

'Let me give you some tea.'

'No, no. I've the dogs to exercise, and Henry wants me to type a talk he's giving in Caxley.'

'It was good of you to come, and kinder still to help with my pinning up. You must bring your husband to meet mine before long.'

She accompanied Mrs Mawne to the front door.

'How do you get on with the next door folk?' asked Mrs Mawne in a voice which was much too loud for Diana's peace of mind. Through one hedge she could see Mrs Fowler, bent to weed her path, but strategically placed to see and hear all that transpired. Intermittent coughing came from beyond the other hedge where Sergeant Burnaby sat enjoying the sunshine. His hearing, for so venerable a man, was amazingly acute at times, as Diana well knew.

'Very well. Very well indeed,' said Diana firmly. 'We're extremely lucky.'

'Glad to hear it. Neighbours can be a curse or a comfort,' boomed Mrs Mawne. She dropped her voice a trifle and spoke now in a tone which was possibly more penetrating than before. 'You'll have to watch Mrs Fowler. A very awkward woman, I hear, and apt to be vindictive. Not to be trusted. Not to be trusted at all. Remind me to tell you a tale next time we meet. More in the nature of a *warning*, you understand.'

'Thank you again for calling,' said Diana. 'I shall look forward to seeing you at the WI meeting.'

Mrs Mawne stumped off to the gate, and Diana watched her departure with relief. The bent figure next door straightened itself with a loud sniff, and the banging of Mrs Fowler's front door seemed to prove the point of the old adage that eavesdroppers hear no good of themselves.

The WI meeting did not take place for a week or more, but before that event occurred Diana met a great many more of Fairacre's inhabitants.

The village shop, which was also the bakery, proved to be as much a club as a business, and here she was introduced to other customers.

The owner was an old boy of Caxley Grammar School and knew Peter well. Old boys were ubiquitous within a radius of ten miles around Caxley and turned up as electricians, plumbers, nurserymen, as well as bank managers, solicitors, accountants and other men of business. The family feeling engendered by this tie was very reassuring, Diana found.

Mr Willet was one of the first friends she met at the shop.

'I'm going your way,' he said on the first occasion. 'Give us your basket, while you carry the cornflakes. That's one's work alone, them great packets.'

They walked amicably along the village street.

'That's my place,' said Mr Willet. 'You must meet my wife some time. She tells me you're going to join the WI.'

'Yes, I am.'

'Jumble-jam-and-Jerusalem!' commented Mr Willet, with a rumbling laugh. 'That's what they calls it, eh? Well, keeps you ladies out of mischief, I suppose. You want to watch they don't get you on the committee though. Fair sharpens their knives there, I understand.'

'Oh, I haven't been here long enough for that honour,' said Diana.

'It's the new ones that get copped,' replied Mr Willet shrewdly. 'You take a look round. You won't find many of the old sort running things in Fairacre – they're too fly. They likes to sit back and watch the newcomers make a mess o' things, and then they can criticize.'

They approached Tyler's Row and slowed to a halt.

'You all right for help in the house?' asked Mr Willet solicitously.

'At the moment, yes, thank you. Mrs Jones who worked for me in Caxley comes out once a week.'

'Good. 'Tisn't easy to get a decent body as you can trust.' He handed over the basket. 'Well, I must be off to the school. Caretaker, see. Odd job man, like. Be plenty of coke spread about the playground for me to sweep up, I've no doubt. Still, did the same meself when I was there fifty years back.'

He gave a smile which creased his weathered face, reminding Diana of a wrinkled apple.

'If you wants anything, let me know. Or your husband now, if he needs a load of logs or someone to fix that gate of yourn, tell him to come and see me. I've heard plenty about him from my two nephews as goes to his school. They've got more up top than I had at their age.'

'I very much doubt it,' said Diana with conviction.

On the following afternoon Diana went to Caxley, and returned to Tyler's Row to find that the first salvo had been fired in a battle which was to last for months.

A light breeze was blowing, and Diana had noticed faint wisps of smoke drifting from the Sergeant's garden across their own, towards Mrs Fowler's property. The bonfire was at the end of the garden, and could have given no offence to anyone, at the stage when Diana first saw it.

She was just peeling off her gloves, when the knock came at the front door. On opening it, she was confronted by Mrs Fowler, dressed very neatly in an afternoon frock, and surmounted by a hat. It was of a masculine nature, something of a trilby modified for feminine wear, but still uncompromisingly severe. Beneath it, Mrs Fowler's grim countenance appeared more formidable than ever.

'Will you come in?' said Diana, regretting the invitation the moment she had made it.

She showed her visitor into the sitting room, and both perched on the edge of their chairs. Mrs Fowler wasted no time.

'I'm here to make a complaint,' she said formally. Her quick eyes were flickering about the room, noting everything. She would be the winner at any Kim's game, thought Diana, with wry amusement.

'I'm sorry to hear that,' she replied. 'Have we done something to offend you, Mrs Fowler?'

'It's not you, ma'am. It's 'im!'

She jerked a thumb at the dividing wall, in the direction of Sergeant Burnaby's abode.

''E does it for sheer devilment,' she went on, her face becoming flushed. 'Waits till 'e sees it 'anging out, then gets to work.'

'Sees what?' asked Diana, understandably bewildered.

'The washing. The clothes. Waits till I've pegged out the lot, and then lights 'is bonfire. Time and time again it's 'appened. All over smuts, they get, clear-starched, fresh-boiled, hand-washed woollies – 'e don't care.'

Diana had often heard of people bridling, and had never quite known what this meant. Now she saw it in action. Mrs Fowler fairly bubbled over with her grievances, but with an air of militancy which boded no good to any who crossed her path just then.

'Surely,' she began gently, 'he doesn't do it intentionally?'

'Oh, don't 'e!' exclaimed Mrs Fowler vindictively. ''E watches the weather-cock on the church to see when 'is ol' bonfire can do most damage! I've seen 'im at it.'

'Then why not go to him and put your complaint directly? What can I do?'

'Well, he's your tenant, same as I am. 'E takes no notice of what I say. Laughs in me face, 'e does. But if you – or, say, Mr Hale – should have a word with the old devil – pardon my language, ma'am – there's a chance 'e might see reason.'

Diana sighed. 'I don't like it at all, Mrs Fowler. We all live at close quarters, and we simply must be understanding and tolerant.'

'I've been that long enough,' retorted Mrs Fowler, buttoning up her mouth.

'Well, I'll tell my husband that you called,' said Diana, rising to her feet, 'but I don't promise that he will intervene. I still advise you to mention the matter politely to Sergeant Burnaby. It's probably just male thoughtlessness. After all, he's getting very old, you know.'

'It's the old 'uns,' said Mrs Fowler darkly, as she crossed the threshold, 'as is the worst!'

'Bad-tempered old harridan,' was Peter Hale's comment that evening when he arrived home from school and was told the tale.

'Let them get on with it. We're not taking sides. Anyway, it's only a storm in a tea-cup. That woman's liverish. You can see that plain enough from her complexion. What she needs is more exercise. A sharp three-mile walk daily would soon put her right.'

'I'll leave you to tell her that,' commented Diana dryly.

10. AWKWARD NEIGHBOURS

No more was heard of this incident, and as Sergeant Burnaby refrained from lighting a bonfire during the next few days, Diana hoped that all would be well. Fairacre was so lovely in the May sunshine that nothing could daunt her spirits for long. They soared even higher when Bert told her that they reckoned to be finished in a week.

'Marvellous!' cried Diana, with heartfelt relief.

'Been a nice job, this has,' said Bert, turning up the transistor's volume a trifle.

'That's right,' shouted Frank, above the racket. 'Peaceful out here. I like a bit of country myself.'

'What say?' bellowed Bert, climbing the stepladder.

Frank executed a few intricate dance steps round a paint pot and ended up nearer his friend.

'Eh?'

'I said "What say?"' repeated Bert, fortissimo.

'Dunno what you're on about,' yelled Frank cheerfully, moving on a yard or two, and beginning to ply his brush languidly.

Diana retreated from the din, savouring this most welcome news. At last, to have the house to themselves!

She told Peter as soon as he came in.

'Now that', he said approvingly, 'calls for a glass of sherry. And it will give me strength to tackle Form One's History essays.'

His glass was empty, and the pile of exercise books reduced by half, when he sat back, sighing. 'Do they teach spelling these days?'

'I think so. Why?'

'Well, it appears from this young man's account of the finding of the treasure ship at Sutton Hoo, that "they discovered golden bowels, spoons and things". What d'you think of that?'

'Odd.'

'Very. Mind you, I must admit to getting a bit tangled with "necessary" and "occurred" myself.

'And "antirrhinum",' agreed Diana thoughtfully.

'Luckily,' said Peter, 'that doesn't seem to crop up very frequently in History.'

He resumed his marking doggedly.

Now that the house was almost straight, the Hales began to entertain their friends. In a cottage as small as theirs, the perfect way to see one's friends was to invite two, or at most four, to dinner.

Diana enjoyed cooking, and the frequent dinner parties which they gave in the early summer evenings gave everyone much pleasure.

The weather was so warm that it was possible to have drinks, and sometimes after-dinner coffee, in the garden. Mrs Fowler and Sergeant Burnaby were interested and not-too-well-hidden spectators on these occasions.

One evening, the Hales had an old college friend of Peter's for the evening. He had been invited to talk to the boys, have tea with the Headmaster, and then drive out to Fairacre.

'Poached salmon?' said Diana. 'Everyone likes it, and if it's cold we needn't hurry with drinks.'

'Fine, fine,' replied Peter, hastily finishing his breakfast.

Diana spent most of the day on her preparations, poaching and skinning the fish, making a green salad, scraping new potatoes, whisking a strawberry mousse, and beating up fresh mayonnaise.

By six-thirty the table was set in the diminutive dining room and Diana awaited their guest. How many years since she had seen Robert, she wondered? The boys had been at school, she remembered. It must be more than ten, though he and Peter had met occasionally during that time.

She dwelt, with some satisfaction, on the meal she had prepared. Everything had gone well. It was bound to be appreciated.

The car arrived and after affectionate greetings, they took their drinks into the garden. The windows of all three cottages stood open. There was no breeze, the air was warm and still, disturbed only by a flight of swifts that were screaming round the village and passed over Tyler's Row, now and again, in their career.

'It's good to be back,' said Robert, his face tilted to watch the birds. 'Do you know it's three years since I've been in England?'

'Is Hong Kong so attractive?'

Robert was in banking and had been abroad for over seven years.

'It is, of course. But it's not that. Somehow I seem to have spent all my leaves elsewhere. My mother and sister are in France now, and I usually go there.'

'How did the boys enjoy your talk?' asked Diana.

'Never seen them so attentive,' said Peter. 'Not since we had that aged general who kept walking about so near the edge of the platform that they held their breath waiting for him to fall off.'

Robert laughed.

'The slides accounted for the attention. Hong Kong is very photogenic. But tell me all the news. How are the boys? And what about the Caxley friends? And how is it working out here? I must say, it all looks marvellous. You've done some good work in this garden.'

'Come and see the vegetable patch,' said Peter, when Robert had finished admiring the flowers. 'Not that we grow much, but Diana thinks a few early potatoes are worthwhile, and lettuces and runner-beans.'

'I grow peas too. Not potatoes though. Never touch 'em. My waist-line won't stand it.'

Diana congratulated herself silently on the large green salad which awaited them. The new potatoes, simmering gently on the stove, would obviously only be eaten by the Hales.

'Sometimes I wonder,' went on Robert, gazing at the young lettuces, 'if exercise helps at all.'

'Of course it does,' said Peter, mounting his hobby-horse. 'Half today's ills are caused through lack of exercise and fresh air.'

'Well, I play golf regularly, and spend a month salmon-fishing with old Craig. Remember him?'

Peter nodded.

'Salmon's rather fattening, I believe,' said Peter.

'I never eat the stuff, anyway,' said Robert. 'Friends get any I catch.'

Peter opened his mouth, caught Diana's eye, and said nothing.

'I must go and dish up,' said Diana, hoping that the tin-opener was in working order. At that moment, the sound of a brass band, energetically playing 'The Turkish March', came from Sergeant Burnaby's windows. The old soldier must have had the volume well turned up, for the rhythm throbbed through the still air, shattering the evening's peace.

'Well, let's hope that soon stops,' commented Peter, watching his wife disappear.

They ate their melon to a musical accompaniment, although the sound was slightly less formidable indoors.

'Ham and tongue,' announced Diana, bearing in the dish.

'Delicious!' said Robert, rubbing his hands together.

Peter said nothing, as he took up the carving knife and fork, but his look of conspiratorial admiration pleased his wife.

Just then, Sergeant Burnaby's radio let forth a prolonged scream, then some whoops, and finally settled down to emit a strident tune with plenty of tympani in evidence. The cottage shook, and a copper bowl on the Hales' mantelpiece began to throb in sympathy.

'I do apologize for this,' said Peter. 'It's worse than it's ever been.'

'Tell me about your neighbours,' said Robert. 'I'm really interested. I never see mine in Hong Kong. I take it one of yours is deaf?'

Diana laughed, grateful to him for the easy way in which he was dealing with the situation. He seemed genuinely amused by the racket next door. Peter, on the other hand, was becoming more furious each minute.

During the strawberry mousse the music changed to a comedy programme of some sort which was interspersed with frequent screams, claps and laughs from what appeared to be a near-demented audience. Sergeant Burnaby's own laughter, punctuated by fits of raucous coughing, could be clearly heard, and added to the general rumpus.

Peter threw his napkin down and pushed back his chair.

'Excuse me. I'd better go and see the old boy. This is unbearable.'

At that moment, they heard Sergeant Burnaby's door being thrown open, the radio blared forth, louder than ever, but above the noise was the shrill screaming of Mrs Fowler's voice. The language was strong, but Sergeant Burnaby, whose voice had been trained in the barrack squares of India, not only shouted her down, but used earthy expressions of Anglo-Saxon origin which were quite new to Diana, but sounded terrifyingly abusive.

'Don't interfere,' said Diana nervously.

Peter's face bore that grim look which generations of youthful sinners had come to fear. 'That's exactly what I'm going to do,' he said ferociously, making for the door.

Within two minutes the voices were silent, the set switched off, and the distant sound of the swifts could be heard again. A bee bumbled against the window pane. Peace had returned.

'Our tenants', said Peter, passing the cheese-board to his guest, 'are something of a problem. Let's hope we'll hear no more of them.'

The evening passed pleasantly, and without further alarms and excursions, but Diana thought it prudent to have coffee indoors after all.

When they had said goodbye to Robert, they returned to the

cottage. An owl was hooting far away, and the scent of early roses hung about the garden like a blessing.

Tyler's Row, quiet now as the grave, looked the epitome of tranquillity.

Peter sighed happily. 'Despite those two, it's a good spot to be,' he commented.

Diana agreed, bending to stroke Tom who was just setting out on his nightly activities. There were far more mice to attend to here than in Caxley. It kept a cat pretty busy, he found.

'By the way,' said Peter, as they mounted the stairs. 'I can get home to lunch tomorrow. Is that all right?'

'Splendid,' said Diana warmly. 'You can guess what it will be!'

Peter's hope that they would hear no more of their tenants was a vain one.

Certainly Sergeant Burnaby's radio set seemed to be put on less frequently, but when it was then the volume was inordinately loud. Diana was positive that the old man's hearing was deteriorating. She had overheard visitors and tradespeople shouting messages at him, in a way which she had not noticed before.

'Well, he'd better get head-phones,' said Peter, when she put forward her suspicions. 'This is no joke.'

Both neighbours were now less friendly to their landlord. Mrs Fowler went indoors, and slammed the door pointedly, if Diana appeared in the garden. Sergeant Burnaby ceased to put his head over the hedge to pass the time of day. Diana found this withdrawal sad, but something of a relief. In any case, there was little she could do.

A week or two after the visit of Robert, a new tactic was tried in the hostilities. Mrs Fowler, more vinegary of countenance than ever, came to the door one evening to complain that the kitchen tap was leaking.

'Needs a new washer, I expect,' said Peter, and in a burst of generosity offered to replace it. Half an hour went by before he returned, looking exasperated.

'I fell into that trap very successfully,' he told Diana. 'Our friend took me all over the house to point out jobs that need doing. The bedroom ceiling needs replastering, two doors have dropped, the rain comes in the spare room window, and something's amiss with the guttering.'

'But you had it looked at when we took over,' protested Diana.

'Maybe she's got grounds for a certain amount of dissatisfaction. I've promised to have a look at these things. Old property wants looking at every week, it seems to me.'

'Was she friendly?'

'Far from it. Frosty, I'd say, with just a hint of a knife up the sleeve somewhere.'

'Oh dear, it is a wretched business! They've been awkward ever since you ticked them off.'

'Well, what do you expect me to do? We do our best not to disturb them. They must do the same.'

Two days later Sergeant Burnaby presented himself at the door and was invited in.

'I hear you're having the workmen along to see to Mrs Fowler's guttering and the window,' said the old soldier. 'Thought it might save them another trip if I showed you the mess the overflow pipe's making down the wall. Wants seeing to badly.'

Peter followed him resignedly.

'What else is wrong?' asked Diana when he came back.

'Damp kitchen floor, stove wants replacing, and the sink's cracked.'

'True?'

'We-e-ll –' drawled Peter, spreading out his hands like a Frenchman, 'nothing's altered since it was inspected three months ago. I can't help feeling that our two tenants are doing their best to get their own back.'

'And what have you told him?'

'The men will come and have another look round. Incidentally, I think you're right about his hearing. He couldn't hear me at all when I was speaking normally. I wonder if the doctor should see him.'

'We shall need to be on better terms before we can broach that subject,' said Diana firmly.

Meanwhile, as the days passed, Diana became convinced that, as with so many deaf people, Sergeant Burnaby heard a great deal more than others imagined.

Mrs Fowler's niece, who lived in Caxley, occasionally came to see her aunt, bringing her two young children with her.

On this particular afternoon, while the women talked over a cup of tea in the kitchen, the children were sent to play in the garden. To Diana, writing the weekly letters to her sons abroad, the sound of their chattering and laughter was very pleasant. Sergeant Burnaby evidently found it otherwise, for, to Diana's astonishment, she heard his voice bellowing across the garden.

'Keep them bloody kids quiet, will you? Get 'em indoors!'

Immediately, he was answered by Mrs Fowler. 'You mind your own business. They make less noise than you do. And get indoors yourself.'

'Fat lot of good trying to get a nap with that row goin' on.'

Another female voice now joined the battle. 'I can look after my own kids, thank you, without any help from you. Just a trouble-maker. I knows you!'

'*Trouble-maker!*' shouted the old soldier, and broke into a terrible fit of coughing.

Diana felt that it was time she asserted herself. This was the first occasion on which the battle had been carried on across her premises, and it was going too far. She emerged from the cottage and approached the two furious women. They looked startled to see her, and Diana suspected that they had thought she was out.

'If you've anything to say to Sergeant Burnaby, please go to see him. *Don't* shout across my garden. It's extremely disturbing.'

'Sorry, I'm sure,' said Mrs Fowler insolently, but she turned to go indoors and the children and their mother followed her.

Sergeant Burnaby, still coughing, and scarlet in the face, peered over the hedge.

'I advise you to go indoors and calm down,' said Diana. 'You are only making yourself worse by flying into such a temper. If you want to speak to Mrs Fowler don't do it across our premises.

'That old besom', gasped the sergeant, 'eggs them kids on to make a row. Does it for spite. She knows I has a nap afternoons. If it's not children, it's that damn dog of hers.'

Still spluttering, he stumped indoors, and Diana watched him go with a sinking heart. The dog, an attractive mongrel bitch, was a new acquisition next door, and Diana had wondered how soon this would be yet another bone of contention. Obviously, Sergeant Burnaby was going to be alert to any little misdemeanours on the dog's part which might be an excuse for further battles.

She went indoors, finished the second letter and read it through, but her mind was elsewhere. It harked back to the quiet privacy of the garden at the old house.

There had been neighbours there, but at four times the distance, and they had been people who behaved in an adult and civilized way. To be in the cross-fire of two such opponents as Mrs Fowler and Sergeant Burnaby, barely twenty or thirty yards apart, was as frightening as it was exhausting. Life at Tyler's Row was going to be impossibly difficult if this sort of conduct continued. Diana had never quarrelled with anyone in her life. This ever-increasing hostility made her acutely unhappy.

She stamped her letters abstractedly. In them she had dwelt on the pleasant side of life at Tyler's Row, the flowers now blooming, the friends who had called, village activities and news of the family. There was no point in burdening the boys with her growing doubts about the wisdom of the move. It would be disloyal to Peter and, in any case, the neighbours were really the only fly in the ointment.

There was one other matter which Diana kept to herself, but one which she knew she must tell Peter before long. For the past few days this fear had haunted her so terribly that she had tried to evade making a decision.

A mole on her neck which had been there for several years was beginning to grow at an alarming rate. She noticed it first as she was drying herself after a bath. It seemed slightly painful and definitely larger than usual. She watched it anxiously for the next three or four days, and was now positive that it was growing steadily. Could it be malignant? Could it be cancerous? She knew so little about these things, but remembered reading somewhere that moles sometimes became a menace.

She knew quite well that she must go and see the doctor. He would probably allay her fears, and if he could not, then the sooner the wretched thing was removed the better.

It was telling Peter which worried her so much. As a family they had all been so wonderfully healthy that any kind of illness seemed doubly horrifying to them. No doubt, thought Diana, with a wry smile, Peter would prescribe a good walk to scotch her trouble.

He had enough to think about, in all conscience. Tyler's Row had cost more than at first estimated, as is usual. The problem of their irascible tenants was going to grow, and he was anxious, Diana knew, that she should settle happily.

Well, one could not arrange these things, thought Diana, taking up her letters. Illness struck without warning. She had lived with this fear now for a week. She must not delay further.

This evening she would share the problem with Peter and make an appointment with their doctor first thing in the morning.

She stood up and looked into the sunlit garden. The single roses were wide open in the heat, showing their golden stamens. A yellow and orange butterfly fluttered over a lavender bush, and a blackbird scratched busily under the lilacs.

It was so beautiful. How could she bear to be taken from it? And how would Peter manage if she died?

Her vision was suddenly blurred by tears, and she pulled herself together. No more morbid thoughts, she told herself. Indulging in self-pity helped no one. She would take her letters and walk in the sunshine to Mr Lamb's Post Office to calm herself.

But a line of poetry throbbed in her head as she walked beneath the trees up to the village:

> Look thy last on all things lovely
> Every hour . . .

and, despite the sunshine, Diana was shaken with the chill of fear.

11. A VILLAGE QUIZ

'I warn you,' said Mr Willet, one June morning, 'Mrs Pringle's comin' up the village street draggin' her leg.'

'Oh, no!' I cried, my heart sinking. 'What's wrong, then?'

'Didn't you ask her to pull out that cupboard to see if there was a mouse there?'

'I asked her to have a look when she swept – yes!'

'Well, she did, and there was, and she says she's strained herself.'

This was dispiriting news. If Mrs Pringle feels that too much has been asked of her, which is a frequent occurrence, then it has dire consequences upon her bad leg. This limb reflects the state of Mrs Pringle's temper and martyrdom as surely as a weather-cock shows the prevailing wind. It 'flares up', as Mrs Pringle puts it, at the slightest provocation. Any little extra effort, such as moving a cupboard, aggravates this combustible quality of her leg, and we all behave with circumspection when Mrs Pringle appears with a limp.

'Let her get on with it,' advised Mr Willet sturdily. 'Pretend you don't notice it, silly old faggot.'

At that moment the door-scraper clanged, and Mrs Pringle appeared over the threshold.

'Lovely morning,' I ventured, with forced cheerfulness.

Mrs Pringle advanced, limping heavily, her head thrust forward like a bull whose patience is fast running out.

'Not if you're In Pain,' boomed Mrs Pringle.

'I'm sorry to hear that,' I replied mendaciously.

Mr Willet looked out of the window, smirking quite unnecessarily.

'I've tore my back muscles and my bad leg, pushing that great cupboard to one side last night. Not that it wasn't needed. That mouse must've been there for weeks. He'd got a fair collection of nuts and berries and rubbish off of the nature table. You know what I'm always saying. That nature table's an open invitation to pests. Stands to reason mice is going to come in for that stuff, spread out for them to help themselves.'

I know quite well, and Mrs Pringle knows that I know, that it is not the mice she dislikes, but the extra debris which the nature table sheds occasionally on to the floor, and which makes more work for her. Mrs Pringle's leg was badly affected on the day some branches of blackthorn capsized, sprinkling the floor heavily with petal confetti.

'What's more,' went on Mrs Pringle remorselessly, 'he's had the corner off of one of them map things. That one with the gentleman made of india-rubber.'

This I rightly construed as the wall chart showing 'The Muscles of The Human Body', an alarming diagram which has not been in use very much since my arrival at Fairacre school. As far as I was concerned, the mouse was welcome to it, but I forebore to say so.

'He's been and chewed it up to shreds so it's no good hopin' to fix it back on, or cryin' over spilt milk.'

'I'm not,' I assured her.

'I shall have to take things easy today,' announced Mrs Pringle, putting a large mauve hand on the small of her back – if so extensive an area of anatomy can be thus called – and limping towards the door.

Mr Willet watched her go solemnly, turned to give me a sympathetic wink, and followed her into the lobby.

A minute later, presumably in the lady's absence, I heard one boy call out: 'You wants to watch it! Ma Pringle's leg's 'urting 'er. You'll get the back of 'er 'and if she sees you doing that!'

The retort was in terms more suited to the public bar of The Beetle and Wedge than the playground of a Church of England primary school.

I decided that I had not heard it.

The days that followed were still darkened by Mrs Pringle's gloomy mood, but the limping seemed to ease a little as the days went by, and we became cautiously hopeful.

The high spot of the week was a visit from Amy. She brought with her a niece of James's called Vanessa, an eighteen-year-old dressed fashionably in a motley collection of shapeless woollen garments in shades of mauve, grey and black. Three sleeves overlapped, the first layer appearing to be some sort of garment which my mother would have called a spencer, then another three-quarter length one, topped by a cardigan which reached the knees but, surprisingly, had short sleeves.

A dull brown stone on an inordinately long silver chain swung over her attire and hit her teacup every now and again when she tossed back a mane of long black hair. The stone reminded me of one shown me once by Mrs Pringle. She had told me, with much relish, that it came from her mother's gall bladder and was much treasured in the family. I am a squeamish woman, and have never quite got over this shattering experience. To have Vanessa's stone swinging about the tea-table was very unnerving.

She was a silent girl, ate very little, and appeared thoroughly bored with our company. As soon as tea was over, Amy dispatched her to the village stores to buy some cigarettes.

'Sorry about this,' said Amy, 'but she's in love. Eileen, James's sister, is at the end of her tether, and I said I'd have her for a few days.'

'What's he like?'

'Unsuitable.'

'How unsuitable?'

'Well, do you remember dear Joyce Grenfell's sketch where the bewildered mother says: "Daddy and I are delighted that you are going to marry a middle-aged Portuguese conjurer, darling. But are you sure he will make you happy?" It's rather like that.'

'Married?'

'Four times already. Has six children, one eye and a cork leg.'

'You're making it up!'

'Cubs' honour!' said Amy, drawing a finger across her throat for added measure. 'May I slit my throat, if I tell a lie, and all that. He was wounded in a war in Bolivia.'

'This gets more unbelievable every minute.'

'It's gospel truth, darling. He recently came as a rep, to the firm where she fiddles with the typewriter all day – one can't call it proper typing. She offered to do some letters for me yesterday, and every one began: "Dear Mr Who-ever-it-was Halfpenny".'

'She has my sympathy,' I said.

'Maybe. You taught yourself, but Vanessa had over a year at some ruinously expensive place in town where she met dozens of perfectly normal cheerful young men of her own generation. But no – she must fall for Roderick.'

'I suppose Eileen's talked to her?'

'Till she's blue in the face. So have I. It makes no difference. She eats next to nothing, dissolves into tears, has constant headaches, and threatens to do away with herself.'

'Can't she change her job?'

'She doesn't want to. She can see the wretched fellow this way. I've offered to take her abroad for a few weeks – James is willing – but Eileen's doubtful and, to tell the truth, I don't know if I could stand it, after having her at close quarters these last few days.'

'What is she interested in?'

'Roderick.'

'I know, silly. But besides Roderick?'

'More Roderick,' said Amy emphatically. 'I tell you, my dear, that child has absolutely no other thought in her head at the moment. Her parents, at their wits' end, have offered her a car, hoping she would find some other interest, but she's even refused that! Have you ever heard of an eighteen-year-old turning down a car?'

'Never!'

'That shows you. Incidentally, James pranged ours last week. He rang up to tell me, and of course I said, "Are you all right?" and I couldn't think why he laughed so much. Evidently, a man in his office always maintains that wives always say this on these occasions. If the *wife* rings up, of course, after an accident, the husband always says: "Is the *car* all right?" So we ran true to form.'

Vanessa appeared in the doorway, holding the cigarettes.

She handed them to Amy without a word, and sank, ex-hausted, into an armchair.

Amy and I stacked the tray and I carried it into the kitchen.

'Come and see the pinks,' I said. 'Would Vanessa like to come in the garden?'

'I should leave her,' said Amy, and so we wandered together down the path, enjoying the June sunlight and the heady scent from the cottage pinks.

'I really can't see why love is cracked up so much,' I said thoughtfully. 'As the Provincial Lady once said, good teeth and a satisfactory bank balance are really much more rewarding.'

'You always were cold-blooded,' said Amy. 'I can remem-ber how you treated that poor young fellow at Corpus Christi when we were at college.'

'If you mean that sanctimonious individual with a name like Snodgrass or Culpepper who was going to be a missionary, he deserved all he got. He was simply looking for someone to accompany him to the poor unsuspecting head-hunters in Africa. Anyone strong and female would have done. Of course I turned him down! So did about a dozen more.'

'Not as flatly as you did. I think you are the most unromantic woman I've ever met.'

'Maybe,' I said, threading a pink in her button-hole, 'but when I meet the Vanessas of this world – and many of them years older, and with less excuse for such follies – then I am sincerely thankful that I am a maiden lady, and likely to remain so.'

Amy laughed indulgently, and we went back to the house to collect her comatose niece. She drifted to the car behind her aunt but, once inside, remembered her manners sufficiently to thank me in a listless voice.

As Amy searched for her car key, Vanessa made her first voluntary contribution to the conversation. There was even a faint hint of animation in her tone.

'What a pretty village this is!'

Amy's mouth dropped open in astonishment. It was good to see her smitten dumb for once. It so rarely happens.

A few days after the visit of Amy and the lovelorn Vanessa, the next meeting of Fairacre Parent–Teacher Association took place.

As I had feared, these monthly meetings seemed to occur much too frequently, and I had reason to dread the present one rather more than usual, for I had agreed, in an off-guard moment, to be on the panel of a question-and-answer session, to be run on the lines of the popular radio programme 'Any Questions?'.

'The vicar will take the chair,' Mrs Johnson told me, 'and you and I will be the female pair of the quartet. Basil Bradley and Henry Mawne are willing to come too, so I think we shall be a well-balanced team.'

Basil Bradley is our local celebrity, a writer who produces

an historical novel yearly. The plot is much the same each season: a Regency heroine, all ringlets and dampened muslin, having an uphill time of it with various love affairs and disapproving parents and guardians, and a few dashing bucks in well-fitting breeches and high stocks, rushing about the countryside at breakneck speed on barely-schooled horses, trying to win her hand, or to stop someone else from winning it.

He sells thousands of copies, is much beloved by many women – and his publisher – and we are very proud of him indeed. He is a gentle, unassuming soul, given to pink shirts and ties with roses on them. The men tend to be rather scornful about Basil, but he is a great deal more astute than his somewhat effeminate appearance leads one to believe.

'We're very lucky to get him,' I said to Mrs Johnson.

'I caught him at the end of a chapter,' she said. 'He was feeling rather relaxed.' She sounded smug, as well she might. Basil Bradley is adept at eluding such invitations.

On the great night, I put on my usual black, with Aunt Clara's seed pearls, and was glad that Amy was not there to protest at my dowdy appearance. With her words in mind, I took a second look at myself in the bedroom mirror. She was right. I did look dreary.

I routed out a shocking pink silk scarf, brought back from Italy by a friend, and tied it gipsy-fashion round my neck, putting Aunt Clara's seed pearls back in their shabby leather case. Greatly daring, I put on some pink shoes bought in a Caxley sale, and took another look at myself. A pity Amy wasn't coming, I thought.

Feeling like the Scarlet Woman of Fairacre, and rather enjoying it, I picked my way carefully across the playground to the school where the quiz was to be held. All the village had been invited, and the place was full.

Mrs Pringle was just inside the door. Her disapproving gasp, on viewing my unaccustomed finery, raised my spirits still higher. Mr Willet, arranging chairs on the temporary platform, gazed at me with open admiration.

'Well, Miss Read,' he said, puffing out his moustache, 'you certainly are a livin' doll tonight.'

I began to have slight qualms. As someone once said: 'No one minds being thought wicked, but no one likes to appear ridiculous.' But I had no time for doubts. The other members of the team arrived, and we took our places meekly.

Basil Bradley, who sat beside me, easily outshone me sartorially. His suit was dove-grey, his shirt pale blue, and his colossal satin tie matched it perfectly. His opposite number, Henry Mawne, was in his church suit of dark worsted, and Mrs Johnson had on a green clinging jersey frock which could have done with a firm corset under it. The vicar, in the chair, looked as benevolent as ever in one of his shapeless tweed suits well known to all in the parish.

Having introduced us, 'just in case there is anyone here who has not had the pleasure of meeting our distinguished panel', the vicar called for the first question. Mrs Johnson had sternly told us that she was not letting us know the questions before-hand, which I thought rather mean of her, so we were all extremely apprehensive about the questions which, no doubt, would be hurled at us like so many brick-bats.

We need not have worried. As with most village affairs, any invitation to speak in public, 'making an exhibition of meself', as Fairacre folk say, was greeted with utter silence and a certain amount of embarrassed coughing and foot-shuffling.

At last, when the vicar could bear it no longer, he pointed to one of the young mothers in the front row, who was clutching a shred of paper which looked suspiciously like a page torn from the laundry book.

'Mrs Baker, I believe you have a question?'

The young woman turned scarlet, stood up, and read haltingly from the laundry book's page.

'How much pocket money do the team think children should get?'

We were all rather relieved at such a nice straightforward question to open the proceedings. Knowing Mrs Johnson, I strongly suspected her of planting a few questions about the hall on such knotty subjects as Britain's role in the Common Market, the rights of parents concerning their children's education, or the part played by the established church in village life.

Henry Mawne was invited to speak first by the vicar. He was admirably succinct.

'Not too much. Give 'em some idea of the value of money. I had a penny a week till I was ten. Then tuppence. Bought a fair amount of hardbake toffee or tiger nuts, tuppence did.'

The mention of tiger nuts brought some nostalgic comments from the older members of the audience, and the vicar was obliged to rap the table for order.

I was next and said that I felt sure it was right to grade pocket money according to age, and that as children grew older it might be a good idea to give them a quite generous fixed amount, and let them buy some of their clothes.

Mrs Johnson felt that there should be a common purse for all the children in the family, each taking from it what was needed, thus training them in Unselfishness and General Cooperation.

This was greeted in stunned silence, broken at last by the vicar who observed mildly that surely a greedy child might take it all in one fell swoop, which would be a bad thing?

'In that case,' answered Mrs Johnson, 'the other siblings' disgust and displeasure would bring home to the offender the seriousness of his mistake.'

'Wouldn't 'ave worked in our house,' said a robust voice from the hall, and the vicar turned hastily to Basil Bradley, who contributed the liveliest theory that children appreciate material things so keenly that it was vitally necessary for them to have enough to enjoy life. His passionate descriptions of the joys of eating dairy-flake chocolate stuffed into a newly-baked bun and eaten hot brought the house down.

We were then asked if we approved of corporal punishment in schools. The men said 'Yes' and gave gruesome accounts, much embellished, I suspect, about beatings given them at school, both ending on the note: 'And I'm sure I was all the better for it!'

Mrs Johnson abhorred the whole idea, and thought infliction of bodily pain barbaric. It simply encouraged sadism in those in authority and, she implied darkly, there was quite enough of that already.

I said that I thought most people found that there were a few hardened sinners for whom the cane was the only thing they feared. Thus I should like to see the cane kept in the cupboard. The mere fact that it was there was a great deterrent to mischief-makers. I added that in all my years at Fairacre I had never had to use it, but that I thought the total abolition of corporal punishment was a mistake.

There was so much interest in this question that it was thrown open to discussion, much to the pleasure of the four of us on the platform, who were then relaxed enough to blow our noses, look at our wrist watches and, in my case, loosen the shocking pink scarf which, though dashing, was deucedly hot.

Mr Willet held the floor for a good five minutes describing his old headmaster's methods at Fairacre school.

'Mr Hope give us a good lamming with the cane whenever he thought it was needed,' he ended, 'and it never done us a 'aporth of 'arm. Boys needs the strap to teach 'em right from wrong. Look at Nature,' he exhorted us. 'Look at a bitch with pups, or an old stag with a young 'un playing up. They gives a cuff or a prod where it hurts, and the young 'uns soon learns.'

There was considerable support for Mr Willet, and it would appear that, in our neck of the woods at least, most of us favour a little corporal punishment in moderation.

We then romped through such questions as: 'Does the team approve of mini-skirts?' Answer: 'Yes, if the legs are all right.'

'Are we doing enough about pollution?' Answer: 'No' – this very emphatically from Henry Mawne, who expatiated on the state of the duck-pond near his house, and the objects he had picked up in the copse at the foot of the downs, for so long that the vicar had to pass to the next question rather quickly.

Reading methods, the debatable worth of psychiatric reports on difficult children, nursery schooling, pesticides, subsidies to farmers, the team's pet hates and where they would spend a holiday if money were no object, were all dealt with, before a halt was called, and we were allowed to totter down from the platform to be refreshed with coffee and a very fine collation of tit-bits prepared by the ladies of the committee.

Mr Johnson offered me a plate, and a paper napkin with Santa Claus and some reindeer on it. Obviously someone had over-estimated the number needed last Christmas. I was glad to see that they were not being wasted.

'I was very glad to hear your remarks about corporal punishment,' he said, in a low voice.

I stared at him, too astonished to reply. My impression had been that he was, if anything, more bigoted than his wife about such things.

'My wife feels very strongly about correction, or rather, non-correction, but there are times when I wonder if a quick slap on the arm or leg isn't a better way of dealing with disobedience or insolence than a rather lengthy discussion. Children aren't always reasonable, I find. Now and again, I must admit, I have doubts.'

'They do you credit, Mr Johnson,' I assured him. 'They do indeed.'

I raised my coffee cup and looked across at him with new respect.

Perhaps, after all, a Parent–Teacher Association had its good points.

12. A Fateful Day

On the last day of June, Diana drove to Oxford by herself. There she had an appointment with a specialist at two-thirty, for although her own doctor had been most reassuring, he was taking no risks.

Peter, much alarmed by Diana's disclosure, had wanted to come with her to the appointment, but she had dissuaded him. She always preferred to face such crises alone. It was less exhausting than trying to put on a brave front in the presence of someone else. Frightened though she was, she wanted to tackle this in her own way, without the effort of calming another's fears as well as her own.

She decided to go in the morning, do a little shopping, have a quiet solitary lunch and have plenty of time to drive to north Oxford where the specialist had his surgery.

Two days of heavy rain had left the countryside fresh and shining. The sun was out as Diana drove away from Fairacre, turning the wet road to black satin, and sparking a thousand miniature rainbows from the raindrops on the hedges. Steam rose from the backs of the sheep as they grazed on the downs, and little birds splashed in the roadside puddles. There was a clean sweetness in the morning air, as the sun gained in strength, and Diana wound down the window of the car, revelling in the freshness. How could one be despondent on such an exhilarating day? How could anything go wrong?

Her mind, suddenly anxious, turned back to the household details. Had she locked both doors? Had she switched off the cooker and the kettle? Had she left water as well as milk and fish for Tom? Had she remembered to put out the bread bin with a note to the baker? Was the shed unlocked so that the laundryman and the butcher could leave their deliveries? Had she put her cheque-book in her handbag, and the shopping list and the card giving particulars of her appointment? Really, going out for the day demanded a great deal of physical and mental activity before it even began, thought Diana! Perhaps she was getting old. As a young thing, she could not remember making such heavy weather over such simple preparations.

This brought her mind back to the nagging worry which had been her constant companion for the last week or two. Could life really be so cruel? Would there be months of pain to face? Death, even? Just as retirement was in sight, and all the simple pleasures that that promised? How truly dreadful suspense was! If only she knew – even the worst could not be more torturing than this gnawing anxiety and apprehension. Well, today might supply the answer. She put her foot on the accelerator and sped forward to her fate.

Oxford's parking problem was as formidable as ever. Diana did the usual round stoically. The car park opposite Nuffield College showed its FULL sign smugly. So did Gloucester Green's. A slow perambulation of Beaumont Street and St Giles showed a solid phalanx of cars, with not one space to be seen. Broad Street appeared equally packed, but to Diana's relief a large bearded man entered an estate car, grinned cheerfully at her to show he was about to go, and drove away, leaving her to take his place gratefully.

The sun had dried the pavements, but the battered heads of the Roman emperors outside the Sheldonian still had one wet cheek where the sun had not yet reached it, and roofs in the shade still glistened with moisture. The city had a freshly-washed air, and a glimpse through the gates of Trinity at the cool beauty of the grass made Diana decide to collect a picnic lunch later on and take it into the hospitable grounds of St John's.

She bought some knitting wool in Elliston & Cavell's, a pair of white sandals in Cornmarket and wandered round the market, enchanted as ever with the bustle and variety. While she was busy in these small affairs her fears were forgotten, but when she stopped for a cup of coffee at Fullers, they came crowding back again, as sinister as a cloud of black bats. If only she knew, if only she knew!

She made herself walk briskly back to the car to deposit her shopping, doing her best to conquer her fears. She would make her way to the Ashmolean. There, among the treasures of centuries, she knew she would find peace. To be in their presence, in the tranquillity of the lovely building, put things in perspective.

On her way she bought a ham sandwich and a banana for lunch. Not exactly a well-balanced meal, she thought with amusement, but easy to handle on a garden seat.

Inside the museum she turned left and made her way to the room she loved most, crammed with a wonderful collection of Worcester china. As usual, it was empty, and Diana sat down on the bench and gazed about her enraptured. There was the set of yellow china she loved particularly, as sunny as prim-roses, as pretty as Spring itself. There were the handsome tureens and plates, the jugs and sauce-boats, which always gave her pleasure. And there was her particular pet – the little white china partridge that she greeted every time she visited the room.

There was something very soothing about these beautiful objects. Perhaps their domestic usefulness, their perfect com-bination of service and splendour was of particular appeal to a woman. Whatever their magic, Diana found it of enormous solace and comfort during that dark hour of anxiety, and she went on her way to St John's in a calmer state of mind.

She walked through the quadrangle to the gardens at the rear. Here it was very quiet. Only the pyracantha petals, falling like confetti over paths and seats, and the fluttering of a few small birds, disturbed the stillness.

The lawns had just been mown. Stripes and swirls across the grass, where the mower had been used, were like gigantic green silk ribbons. In the borders delphiniums and peonies towered, a glory of blue, pink and cream, and in front of them clove pinks sent out their spicy fragrance.

Diana settled herself on a seat in the sun, and took out her ham sandwich. Instantly, a robin appeared, then another and another, until four robins eyed her brightly from very near at hand. She threw them crumbs, relishing their boldness, their soft feathered rotundity, and the swiftness of their movements.

Before long, a few more people wandered into the garden with their packets of lunch. Diana was struck by their general air of happiness. Most of them were women, faces upturned to the sunshine, half-smiling – children again in a world where flowers and birds, quietness and fragrance, took precedence, and one had time to observe, to reflect, to wonder and to be glad.

One middle-aged woman in particular, dressed in a floral summer frock covered by a shapeless cardigan, settled not far from Diana. Her face was so serene, her happiness so apparent, that Diana began to wonder, not for the first time, if women imbibed the atmosphere of a place more quickly than men. Had they a more ready response to surroundings?

A young girl, plain to the point of ugliness, peering through thick glasses between two swinging bunches of matted hair, suddenly knelt down on the damp path by the pinks, her arms crossed over her breast, and bent down to bury her face in them. She looked as though she were making obeisance to beauty, and when she sat back on her heels. Diana saw that her face was transformed. Sheer bliss had made her, suddenly and miraculously, into a beauty.

Diana finished her simple repast, tidied away her rubbish and gave the last few crumbs to the attentive robins who, by now, had been joined by a hopeful band of sparrows. For a few minutes she leant back in the seat, just another middle-aged woman, enjoying the benison of June sunshine on her face, and gave herself over to the peace of the place.

She must have dozed, for when she looked at her wrist

watch she saw that it would soon be two o'clock. Reluctantly, she returned to this world, making her way towards the gate, stopping only to smell a single pink rose by the path. It seemed perfect, its petals translucent in the sunshine, cupping a glory of golden stamens, but, as she bent to smell it, Diana saw a small green grub in its depths, and she drew back with a shudder.

She regained the car, turned its nose northward, with a sinking heart, and began to thread her way through the traffic.

The quiet world was behind her. Now she must face the darker side of reality with what courage she could muster.

The specialist was a tall, lantern-jawed Scotsman, infinitely gentle and reassuring. He examined Diana with concentrated deliberation, and finally told her that the chances of the growth being malignant were slight, but that he would like to have some tests made to make quite sure.

He gave her a card to take to an Oxford hospital in the following week for this to be done, bade Diana a courteous farewell, and accompanied her to her car solicitously.

Another delay, thought Diana, near to tears as she drove home to Fairacre. Another whole week to live through, frightened and apprehensive.

She tried to concentrate on the words of comfort the Scotsman had given her, but doubts kept breaking in. It was very hot now, and the car seemed stifling despite having all the windows open. The distant downs shimmered in the heat. A dog lay panting on a cottage doorstep. His master, sitting on a wooden kitchen chair beside him, dozed with a panama hat tipped forward on his nose. Some children were coming out of school in one of the villages. Even they appeared languid in the brilliant sunshine, drifting along, their hands brushing the long grasses by the hedge, instead of jumping and shouting as children normally do when released from their desks.

For the last few miles of her homeward journey, Diana

deliberately wrenched her mind from her troubles and tried to relive the pleasure of the morning. She thought of the loveliness of rain-washed ancient streets and monuments, the garnered treasures in the Ashmolean, the exquisite beauty, ravishing all the senses, in the garden of St John's.

But always, at the back of her consciousness, was the niggling fear of what might be. It reminded her of that rose – so perfect, it seemed, but with 'a worm in the bud'. A world full of delights was about her, but fear ate her heart, and spoilt perfection.

Peter was home early, waiting to greet her and to hear how she had fared. He shared her dismay at yet more suspense, but did his best to cheer her.

They sat in the garden, under the shade of the old plum tree, and sipped tea. The neighbours were very quiet, and Diana commented on it with relief.

'They weren't half-an-hour ago,' said Peter. 'The old man met me on the doorstep when I got back. He was absolutely furious. It seems that Mrs Fowler's dog got into the garden and buried a bone in his border. Heaven knows it's not all that spick and span! I should have thought he would have welcomed a bit of digging. However, he took umbrage. They evidently had a slanging match during the afternoon, and he was waiting to "complain about my tenant"!'

'What did you do?'

'Told him to forget it. I also told him that we were getting absolutely sick of these upsets, and that he might have to think of finding another place to live if he couldn't come to terms with things here.'

'We certainly can't go on like this,' said Diana.

Tom approached languorously, his tail flicking from side to side. He disliked the heat, but had stirred himself from under the shade of the lilac bushes to investigate the clinking of china and teaspoons. A saucerful of milk was always welcome.

Diana watched him lapping, taking the milk fastidiously

round the edge of the saucer. Her mind dwelt on the scene Peter had described.

She knew why he had been so ruthless this time. He was anxious about her, and determined that nothing which he could prevent should worry her further. She herself could never have brought such pressure to bear on poor old Sergeant Burnaby, but she was glad that the words had been said. Their neighbours were fast becoming the serpent in their little Eden.

'Worms in the bud,' quoted Diana aloud, with a sigh.

'Where?' said Peter. 'I'll get the spray.'

Diana laughed. 'Just a figure of speech. Our neighbours – a canker at the heart of things – spoiling it all.'

Peter looked grim. 'They won't be at the heart of things much longer, if they don't mend their ways. I know we can't give them notice, but I can tell them to mend their ways. They're living on the edge of a volcano, if they did but know it, and it's liable to erupt at any moment!'

'Perhaps they'll heed your words of warning.'

'They'd better,' said Peter shortly.

13. Dog Trouble

'What d'yer think of it?' enquired Mr Willet, proudly holding a small wooden structure before me. It looked like a miniature dog kennel without sides, but I guessed, accurately for once, that it was a rather superior bird-table.

'Lovely!' I replied. 'Did you make it?'

'Yes. It's for Mr Hale. They've got one already, and I copied it for him. Wondered if you could do with one, miss? I've got plenty of wood, and that old one I did you hasn't got a nice little roof like this. Keeps the birds' food nice and dry when it rains, this does.'

'Yes, please. I'd love one.'

'You can 'ave it on a stout pole, or 'ang it up by a bit of chain off of a bracket,' said Mr Willet, warming to his work. 'What say?'

'Give me till tomorrow to decide,' I said, after some thought. 'I'll try and fix on a good spot where I can see it from the house.'

'Fair enough,' agreed my caretaker, lodging the edifice carefully on the side desk which supports everything from models, paintings waiting to dry and large garnered objects such as a sheep's skull from the downs, bleached white and papery, down to packets of biscuits and half-sucked lollipops carefully shrouded in a scrap of grease-proof paper, awaiting their owners' attention at playtime.

'Nice people them Hales,' went on Mr Willet conversationally. 'Friendly, but don't push in, like. For a schoolmaster he's really a very nice chap indeed. I mean, teachers can be funny old things. The women all teeth-and-britches, and the men a bit toffee-nosed, by and large.'

He stopped suddenly, his rosy face turning an even deeper rose with embarrassment. It is not often one sees Mr Willet discomfited. I quite enjoyed the occasion.

'There now!' he exclaimed, slapping his thigh with exasperation, 'I ought to be shot, that I ought. Talk about the tongue being an unruly member! I'm truly sorry I spoke as I done, Miss Read. I meant no offence. You're the last one to call a teeth-and-britches-madam. Why, you looked a fair picture the other night in that pink tippet you had round your throat.'

'You're very kind,' I said, 'and don't bother your head about your very fair assessment of some of my profession. I'm glad Mr Hale passes muster.'

'It'll teach me to guard my tongue. What a thing to say! I'll be hot and cold for weeks every time I remember it!'

'Don't remember it, then. It's not worth worrying over. If I took to heart all the bloomers I've made in my life, I should have slit my throat by now,' I assured him.

'That Mrs Hale now, she's a real lady. Don't look very well to me, though. Always busy in that house, getting it straight, you know, and only that Mrs Jones to help her once a week. They do say she's giving up. Have you heard?'

I said that the grapevine had not extended as far as the school house yet, but no doubt word would reach me before long.

Mr Willet coughed delicately, and looked about him for any eavesdroppers.

'It's like this. *If* Mrs Jones is leaving, my wife would dearly love a little job at Tyler's Row. She's been in good service, as you know, and we're only a few steps away. It would fit in lovely with her own bits of house-keeping. Should I mention it, do you think?'

I felt a rare pang of envy. Mrs Willet is a sweet little mouse of a woman, wonderfully capable at running a home, discreet, kindly – in fact, the proverbial treasure. I should dearly love to have invited her to work for me, but my house is so small, needing only one morning's work a week, and Mrs Pringle, alas, already has the job. It would be open warfare to change the arrangements, even supposing Mrs Willet wished to come. I dismissed the happy dream with a sigh.

'If Mrs Willet's agreeable,' I said, 'I don't see why not. Then it's up to Mrs Hale, if she needs her at any time. I may say, I think she's jolly lucky. There's no one in the village I should like more than your wife to work for me.'

'Well, that's very handsome of you, miss, particularly after all I blurted out just now. Yes, my Alice is pretty good, I must say. Pretty good! I expect she'd like the chance to work for you, but then you're suited, aren't you?'

' "Suited" isn't the word I'd choose,' I told him. 'Let's say I am unable to alter present arrangements.'

'Here comes the old girl now,' said Mr Willet, hurriedly picking up the bird-table. 'You let me know where you wants yours, when you've decided, and I'll be up one evening to fix it up for you.'

'I shall look forward to that,' I told him.

'With a smart contraption like this,' he said, smiling, 'you'll be gettin' all the fowl of the air. Tits, robins, nut-hatches, chaffinches – maybe hoopoes and peacocks!'

'You'd better make it twice the size then,' I shouted after his retreating back.

The week in which Diana Hale waited to go for her hospital tests seemed to be the longest of her life.

Not that it was without incident. Mrs Jones, who had agreed to come once a week 'just to see how it goes', found that the journey made the day a long one, and having expressed her doubts about being able to continue, particularly during the winter, finally gave her notice during the week of waiting.

Both women were genuinely sorry to part. Mrs Jones had been a faithful servant for many years, a staunch friend to the

Hales and their two boys. But she was getting on in years, and Diana could see that she was wise to give up.

'I shan't leave until you've found someone else,' declared Mrs Jones. 'But I thought you should know the minute I'd made up my mind. There'll be plenty in the village, I don't doubt, as would jump at the job.'

'Well, I hope so,' admitted Diana, 'but it will be hard to find someone as reliable as you are.'

She pondered the matter in bed that night, as Peter slept dreamlessly.

Should she advertise in the *Caxley Chronicle*? Or would a postcard put up in Mr Lamb's Post Office be better? Or simply let him know that she was looking for domestic help?

The night was warm, and the smell of jasmine crept sweetly through the open window. Somewhere, across the village, an owl hooted in the darkness. There seemed to be rustling sounds, too, in the garden. Tom, perhaps, stalking a poor mouse, or even hedgehogs on the prowl. They could make quite a lot of noise for such small animals.

Suddenly, the unearthly howling of a dog split the silence, followed by a sharp yapping, and then the unmistakable shindy of a dog fight just below the window. More barking added to the din.

Peter sat up, jerked from slumber. 'What the devil's going on?'

'I don't know. It's only just started.'

Before he had time to get out of bed to investigate, there was the sound of a window opening next door. Mrs Fowler was obviously making her own investigations.

'Push off!' screamed the lady, beside herself. 'Get off home! Be off with you!'

There was the sound of another window opening. Sergeant Burnaby, it seemed, had also been disturbed, despite his deafness.

'Stop that hollering!' commanded the sergeant, in a voice

that had made itself heard under heavy shell-fire in its time. 'How d'you expect law-abiding Christians to sleep with that racket going on?'

'If I had a gun,' said Peter grimly to Diana, 'I'd train it on our neighbours in turn, so help me. As it is, I suppose I'd better lean out and read the riot act.'

'Not for a minute,' begged Diana. Who knows what he might say in the heat of the moment!

'You mind your own business,' yelled Mrs Fowler, evidently retreating for a moment, but returning to her post bearing something that chinked against the window fastening.

The dog-fight seemed to be continuing a little further down the garden, but there were whimpering sounds and more barking near at hand, as if a dozen or more dogs were still close to the house.

A sloshing noise, followed by wild yelping and what sounded like a stampede of elephants, indicated that Mrs Fowler had tipped the water from the bedroom ewer over her unwelcome guests.

'Let that be a lesson to you!' she shouted, slamming shut the window with such force that all four cottages in Tyler's Row shuddered.

There was an answering slam from Sergeant Burnaby's window, and then silence from each side of the Hales' abode. Outside, the noise of snuffling, whining and yelping went on, but with slightly less energy. Mrs Fowler's activity with the water jug seemed to have some effect. Certainly the two main contestants seemed to have retired, probably to carry on their dog-fight in some other quarter of the village.

'I suppose that damn dog of hers is on heat,' said Peter gloomily. 'How long does that last?'

'About three weeks, I believe.'

'That's jolly. I suppose we'll have all the dogs of the neighbourhood growling and prowling round, like the hosts of Midian. Do the garden a power of good, that will!' He sighed gustily. 'I wonder if we've been fools to come here? I must say I never envisaged this sort of persecution when we took on the tenants. What d'you think, Di?'

He sounded unusually downcast, and Diana rallied herself to speak cheerfully, although she too was full of doubts lately.

'It will turn out all right. They are bound to settle down before long. You've told them. It's up to them to have a little sense. I can stand it, if you can. We've put all we can spare into this place, and we'll jolly well see it gives us pleasure – neighbours or not.'

'That's how I feel. I just can't bear to think I've landed you with this lot. After all, I'm out all day. You're the one who has to put up with it, and you've got enough to worry you just now without these two pests.'

'Forget it,' said Diana comfortingly. 'Let's go to sleep.'

To the faint sound of mingled whimpers and snuffles, the Hales sought slumber.

The next morning a collection of dogs of all shapes and breeds were visible through Mrs Fowler's hedge, clustered hopefully at her back door. There were plenty of paw marks on the Hales' garden beds, and two of Diana's cherished penstemons were broken down.

She was understandably nettled, but tried not to show it in front of Peter, who was worried enough anyway. He drove off to school, and Diana set about her domestic chores.

The morning was punctuated by commotions from Mrs Fowler's side of the hedge. Every time she opened the back door, she emerged either with a stick or a jug of water to send off the amorous invaders.

At the same time she let fly a stream of invective which quite unnerved Diana. She wondered how soon it would be before Sergeant Burnaby retaliated.

She did not have long to wait.

A peremptory rapping at the back door came about ten

o'clock. On opening it, Diana faced Sergeant Burnaby, very spruce, his waxed moustache tilted heavenward and his yellow face unusually stern.

'Come in,' said Diana, with a sinking heart.

'Thank you, ma'am. I shan't keep you long. My business won't take more than a minute or two.'

'Do sit down,' invited Diana.

'No, thank you, ma'am. I'll say what I have to say standing. I only come because I respect your wanting to 'ave a bit of dignity over Mrs Fowler's and my upsets. This 'ere bawling that she does is no way to go on.'

Diana, remembering the Sergeant's stentorian bellows in the night, found herself speechless.

'I'm here to lodge a complaint,' went on the old man, 'a *formal complaint*. If your blasted tenant can't keep her blasted bitch under control, I give fair warning I'll take the matter to the police.'

This was said in Sergeant Burnaby's most polite tones, and Diana was hard put to it not to show her amusement.

'Sergeant Burnaby,' she said, in the cooing voice which had melted many men's hearts, 'you are making yourself so unhappy – and us too, you know – by taking offence at every little thing which goes wrong. Of course it's annoying to have all these dogs about, and I intend to visit Mrs Fowler to see what can be done about it. We can't have our sleep broken as we did last night, but *please*, Sergeant, try to be a little more forbearing. We've simply *got* to shake down together peaceably. You must see that.'

Diana thought she detected a little shame in the old soldier's countenance, but his answer was as belligerent as ever.

'I've done my best, ma'am, as you know. That woman's more than flesh and blood can stand, and that damn dog of 'ers has caused my garden to be turned into a fair wilderness with all them others rooting about. I means it when I says I'll see the police!'

Diana put a hand upon his arm pleadingly. 'Now don't do anything hasty. I shall see Mrs Fowler myself. We all want an end to this unpleasantness.'

The old man stumped towards the door, his back as straight as a ramrod, his moustache bristling.

'Well, I've made my complaint. I can't do more. But she'd better watch out!'

Diana abandoned her soft womanliness and assumed a sterner tone. 'Sergeant Burnaby, you must do your part in a little give-and-take. As my husband has told you, if you can't settle happily at Tyler's Row it may be best for you to find somewhere else to live.'

If Diana expected a change of attitude, she was to be disappointed. The old man said nothing, but gave her a glance so full of venom that she felt shocked.

The door slammed behind him. It was plain that Sergeant Burnaby was unrepentant.

Later that day she called upon Mrs Fowler with much the same result. It had needed considerable courage to visit her neighbour, but Diana felt that it must be done.

Eight dogs waited hopefully in the garden, and watched Diana as she approached.

'Better come in, I suppose,' said Mrs Fowler sourly, eyeing the expectant crowd. 'It's about *them*, no doubt.'

She shut the door behind her visitor and motioned Diana to a battered sofa.

'Yes, it is, I'm afraid,' said Diana. 'Not only on our behalf, but on Sergeant Burnaby's as well.'

Mrs Fowler gave a contemptuous laugh. 'Should've thought he could have done his own dirty work.'

Diana decided to ignore this, and pressed on.

'It's very difficult when you have a bitch, I know –' she began.

'I won't have that word mentioned in my house,' said Mrs

Fowler loftily. She folded her arms across her pink cardigan and glared at poor Diana. 'I always say *lady-dog*. It's politer.'

'Just as you wish,' agreed Diana hastily. She was devoutly thankful that Peter was not present, or she might have broken down. 'I just wondered if you knew that there is something available for bitch – I mean, for lady-dogs – which can be put on them when they're on heat. It keeps the dogs away, and is so simple.'

Diana's innocent suggestion brought a blush to Mrs Fowler's withered cheek, but whether it was caused by outraged modesty or plain temper it was difficult to guess.

'I know the stuff. My niece brought me a tin last night.' She turned round to root among a number of medicine bottles and aerosol tins on the dresser, and held up a large yellow canister proudly. Bright red letters across it said: KUM-NOT-NY.

'Haven't had time to use it yet,' went on Mrs Fowler, 'and I don't know as I intend to. Nature knows best, my mother always said.'

Diana, who had now recovered from the shock of the name, decided that a firmer line was needed.

'I should certainly use it *immediately*, or I fear Sergeant Burnaby will be sending for the police. My husband and I are sympathetic to your difficulties, but they can be overcome, and you really can't want to upset your neighbours like this. If you don't want to use this stuff, then why not put the dog into kennels? It's often done.'

Mrs Fowler bridled. 'And who's going to pay for that, may I ask?'

'The dog is your responsibility,' replied Diana steadily. She got up from the little-ease of a sofa, and made her way to the door.

Mrs Fowler looked thoughtful. 'I might have a word with my niece when she brings the children to tea,' she said, in a less belligerent tone of voice.

'Do,' replied Diana. 'And please remember that we all want to sleep at nights – *all of us* – in Tyler's Row.'

Luckily, Diana's words bore fruit. She saw the niece depart, after tea next door, complete with children and the dog. Kum-not-ny must have been applied with a heavy hand, for no dogs followed the little group towards the bus stop, and Tyler's Row was destined to have peaceful nights for over a fortnight.

Diana saw the family waiting for the bus when she went to the Post Office with her carefully written postcard asking for domestic help, on one or two mornings a week, times and wages to be arranged.

'I'll put this up first thing tomorrow,' promised John Lamb. 'I'm sure you'll be suited without much bother.'

He watched Diana depart, and put the card carefully on one side. He must look out for Bob Willet. This was just the job his missus was looking for, he knew. There was not much that John Lamb did not know in Fairacre.

By eight-thirty the next morning, Mr Willet knew about the post as he returned from his early duties at the village school. After a brief word with Mrs Willet, he collected the bird-table and made his way to Tyler's Row. Diana was dusting, but went out into the morning sunshine to admire the bird-table.

'It's really splendid,' she cried. 'Do you want to put it up now?'

'Better wait till Mr Hale's here,' advised Mr Willet. 'I'll call back this evening, if it's convenient. I'll be going up to choir practice and I should be back here by eight or so. Mr Annett's written a descant to "Pleasant are Thy courts above". We're doin' it Sunday.'

'How clever of him,' commented Diana.

'Well, that's as maybe. It's my belief he's tone-deaf when it comes to makin' up tunes. This 'ere fairly pierces yer eardrums. Atonal, he called it. That's one way of describing it, I suppose.'

'Modern music does take some getting used to,' agreed Diana diplomatically.

'I was having a word with John Lamb,' said Mr Willet. 'He tells me as you need a bit of help here. I was wondering if Mrs Willet might come and see you? She's looking for a light job, and you wouldn't get nobody better, and that's the truth.'

Diana gasped with pleasure. She had met Mrs Willet at the Women's Institute, and frequently in the lanes of Fairacre. This seemed heaven-sent.

'This is good news. Would Mrs Willet like to call here soon and have a look at the work? At the moment I am paying Mrs Jones twenty-five an hour. She might like to know.'

'Twenty-five?' said Mr Willet, puzzled.

'New pence.'

'Ah!' Mr Willet's brow cleared. 'Five bob! This decimation gets you down, don't it? By the time I've decimated shillings and pence, I don't know if I'm on my head or my heels. D'you have trouble decimating, Mrs Hale?'

'It's getting easier. It's pints into litres and ounces into grammes I'm dreading.'

'Well, now. What about Mrs Willet comin' next Tuesday, to see the job?'

'Fine,' said Diana, then checked suddenly. 'No, sorry, I have to go to hospital that day.'

She regretted the disclosure the minute she had made it. Mr Willet's face crumpled with concern. She hoped he would not mention the matter to others. However, nothing could be done.

'Nothing serious,' she said lightly. 'Just a routine check.'

'Good. Good,' said Mr Willet, looking relieved. 'Then perhaps Monday would be better?'

'Ideal. Would two o'clock be a good time?'

'Do fine. We've washed up and had a bit of a ziz by then. Forty winks, after a bit of dinner, is a very good thing, Mrs Hale.'

He put the bird-table in the porch, and surveyed it with his head on one side.

'Looks a treat, don't it?' he said disarmingly. 'I enjoyed makin' that.'

'We'll enjoy using it,' Diana told him, with conviction.

PART THREE

Settled, With Some Sunshine

* * * *

14. AMY'S INVITATION

The fact that Diana Hale had to go to hospital was soon general knowledge in Fairacre. To give Mr Willet his due, he mentioned this interesting item of news to his wife alone. Whether she inadvertently let the cat out of the bag, or whether Sergeant Burnaby or Mrs Fowler overheard the conversation in the garden, or whether, as is quite likely, that mysterious communication system, the village grapevine, which works with a life of its own, was to blame, no one can tell, but the village knew quite well that on Tuesday next Mrs Hale was going to hospital.

Why, and which one, were matters of debate. Some said the appointment was at Caxley-Cottage, others Up-the-County, and those who guessed aright plumped for Oxford. These last admitted that there were so many hospitals in Oxford that it was anyone's guess which it would be. By the law of elimination they cancelled out That Bone Place (Orthopaedic) and That Loony Place (Nervous Diseases), on the grounds of Diana's physical activity and her obvious mental composure. Further than that they were unable to go, to their infinite regret.

The reason for the visit engaged the villagers' interest pleasurably. Heart trouble and hernias, goitre and gall-stones, diabetes and deafness were all discussed with lively conjecture, and gruesome accounts of relatives' sufferings when similarly afflicted.

Even the school children discussed the subject, seriously and with sympathy. I overheard two of them as they squatted on their haunches by a sunny wall, waiting to come into school.

'What's up, d'you reckon, with that new lady up Tyler's?'

'Nothin' much. Havin' a baby, I expect.'

'Get away! She's too old. She must be sixty or seventy. My mum says you can't have a baby after forty.'

'That's where she's wrong then. Our mum had our Linda when she was forty-three. So there!'

There was silence for a moment before Mrs Hale's case was resumed.

'Don't expect it's an operation. More like getting old. Bits of you wears out, like an old bike doos.'

'She ain't all that old. Not much more'n Miss Read.'

'Well, *she's* no chicken! I bet she's got bits of *her* wearin' out pretty fast.'

Too true, I thought, tottering into the playground to call them in, I felt decrepit for the rest of the day.

On Wednesday morning Mrs Pringle told me, with evident disappointment, that Mrs Hale had been seen busy weeding the borders on Tuesday evening.

'Can't be much amiss there,' grumbled the lady. Then her eye brightened. 'Unless the doctors have missed something,' she continued. 'Some of these young fellers – no more than bits of boys – simply give you a quick prod here and there, and look at your tongue, and that's it. Easy enough to miss the Vital Symptom.'

'I feel very sorry indeed for Mrs Hale,' I began severely, about to embark on a short pithy lecture on the theme of prying into the affairs of others, but Mrs Pringle forstalled me as successfully as ever.

'Oh, so do I. So do I. There's not one in the village as doesn't feel the same. Mrs Fowler reckons it's liver. Sergeant Burnaby reckons it's a judgement, whatever that may mean, and John Lamb says he's never been one to talk about women's ills and then shut up like a clam!'

'Sensible man,' I said.

'I wonder what that poor soul's doing at this very minute,' pondered Mrs Pringle lugubriously.

'Minding her own business perhaps,' I retorted tartly.

And, for once, I had the last word.

More news came from Tyler's Row within the week. Mrs Willet was going to work for Mrs Hale!

'She's very lucky,' I said feelingly to Mrs Pringle when she told me.

'She is indeed. Five shillings an hour!'

I had meant that Mrs Hale was lucky, and said so.

'Well, yes,' Mrs Pringle conceded doubtfully. 'Alice Willet's a good worker and a very nice little carpet beater, considering her arms.'

Mrs Willet's arms, compared with Mrs Pringle's brawny ones, are certainly rather wispy, but I was not surprised to hear her praised as a carpet beater. As far as I could see, Mrs Willet would be competent at anything she undertook, and I said so.

Mrs Pringle seemed to resent my enthusiasm, and began to look mutinous. Before long, I knew from experience, spontaneous combustion would occur in her bad leg, and we should all suffer.

'Alice Willet,' said Mrs Pringle heavily, 'doesn't have what others have to put up with.'

This barbed remark might have referred to me, or to the children, or to us both, but prudence kept me silent. With only the slightest limp Mrs Pringle made her way to the lobby.

'Don't come walking all over my clean floor with your feet!' I heard her shout to the oncoming children.

'Just walk on your hands,' I said.

But I said it to myself.

During that week I had a surprise visit from Amy. Her car was waiting in the lane as the children left school, and I greeted her warmly.

'Come and have some tea.'

'Lovely. But nothing to eat. I'm getting off a stone and a half.'

'How do you know?'

'Because that is what I *intend* to do,' said Amy sternly, locking the car door – a wise precaution, even in comparatively honest Fairacre.

'Good luck to you,' I said, leading the way to the school house. 'I lose four pounds after three weeks of starvation, and then I stop.'

'Wrongly balanced diet,' began Amy, then stopped dead, listening.

A distant mooing noise came from the direction of the school.

'What on earth's that? One of the children crying?'

'Mrs Pringle singing. She usually practises the Sunday hymns as she sweeps up. That sounds like "Eternal Father strong to save", unless it's Mr Annett's new descant.'

'It sounds to me like murder being done,' said Amy, picking her way carefully across the stony playground to my gate. Her cream suede shoes were extremely elegant, but really too beautiful for walking in.

'I'm starving,' I told her, as I put on the kettle, 'and intend to have a large slice of Dundee cake. Shall I eat it out here in the kitchen to save you misery?'

'No,' said Amy, weakening, 'cut me a slice, too!'

Later, demolishing the cake as hungrily as we used to at college so many years ago, Amy came to the reason for her visit.

'I wanted to tell you the latest news of Vanessa and also to invite you to a little party. I've got such a nice man coming.'

I began to feel some alarm. Every now and again, Amy tries to marry me off to someone she considers suitable for a middle-aged schoolteacher. It is rather wearing for all concerned.

'Who is he?' I asked suspiciously.

'A perfect dear, called Gerard Baker. He writes.'

'Oh lor!'

'Now, there's no need to take that attitude,' said Amy firmly, picking a fat crumb from her lap and eating it with relish. 'Just because you took a dislike to that poor journalist fellow at my cocktail party –'

'A dislike! I was terrified of him. He was a raving lunatic, trying to interview me on Modern Methods of Free Art over the canapés. What's more, his beard was filthy.'

'Well, Gerard is clean-shaven, and cheerful, and very good company. He's writing vignettes of minor Victorian poets.'

'How I hate that word "vignettes"!'

'And he's here for a few weeks,' went on Amy, carefully ignoring my pettish interjection, 'because he is finding out about Aloysius Someone who lived at Fairacre years ago and wrote poetry.'

'What! Our dear old Loyshus? Mr Baker must meet Mr Willet.'

'And what can he tell Gerard?'

'Everything. How his cottage smelt like "a civet's paradise", and how long his poetry readings were – oh, hundreds of things.'

'They don't sound quite the things for vignettes,' said Amy pensively.

'He'll have to call them something different then. I've no doubt he'll work out some horribly whimsical title like "Baker's Dozen".'

'Now, now! Don't be so tart, dear. I know you'll get on very well, and for pity's sake don't wear that black rag. If you can't afford to buy a new frock, I'll he pleased to buy you one.'

'Thank you,' I said frostily, 'but I haven't sunk to that.'

'Hoity-toity!' shrugged Amy, quite unconcerned. 'Friday week then? About six-thirty?'

'Lovely,' I said gloomily. 'Now tell me about Vanessa.'

Amy lit a cigarette luxuriously, put her beautiful shoes up on the sofa, and settled down for a good gossip.

'That wretched man was *married*.'

'I know. Four times. You told me.'

'Yes, but he'd tried to make Vanessa believe that he'd tidied all four away by death or divorce. Actually, he is still married to Number Four. Just think of it! If Vanessa had married him, he would have been a bigamist!'

'How did Vanessa find out?'

'Oh, Somebody knew Somebody, who knew Somebody whose children went to the same school as his and Number Four's. You know what London is – just a bigger Fairacre when it comes to it.'

'Is she very upset?'

'Dreadfully. She can't decide whether to go into a convent or to take up the guitar.'

'I should try the guitar first,' I said earnestly. 'It's not quite so final.'

'I really believe she's beginning to grow out of this awful infatuation at last. At least her mind is turned towards these other two subjects. When she was with me she thought solely of Roderick. There seems to be a ray of hope.'

'Is she coming to the party?'

'Now that's an idea. I think it might be a very good thing. She would meet a few new people, and she liked you, strangely enough.'

'There was no need for the last two words.'

'I suppose there was a fellow feeling,' mused Amy, tapping ash into the fireplace absently. 'Two spinsters, you know.'

'I'm not crossed in love,' I pointed out.

'You might well be, after meeting Gerard,' said Amy smugly. 'We shall have to wait and see.'

*

Term was due to end within three weeks, and already I was beginning to quail at the thought of all the things that had to be done before the glad day arrived.

I had to find out about new entrants to the school in September, when the school year began. There were reports to write, cupboards to tidy, present stock to check, new stock to order, the school outing – a time-honoured trip to the sea with the choir and other church workers – and our own Sports Day, which involved giving refreshments to parents and friends of the school.

It was whilst I was contemplating this daunting prospect that Mrs Bonny dropped her bombshell. She has been a tower of strength ever since her arrival at the school, and in one as small as Fairacre's, with only two on the staff, it is vitally important that the teachers get on together. Mrs Bonny and I had never had a cross word, and I had hoped that she would continue to teach for many years, although I knew there was some doubt when she remarried at Christmas.

She came into the playground as I sheltered in a sunny recess made by one of the buttresses. My mug of tea was steaming nicely, and playground duty was quite pleasant on such a blue-and-white day, with rooks cawing overhead, and the ubiquitous sparrows hopping about round the children's feet, alert for biscuit crumbs.

'Gorgeous day,' I remarked.

'Well – er – yes,' said Mrs Bonny vaguely. She twisted the wedding ring on her plump finger, and I wondered why she appeared so nervous.

'I've something to tell you.'

'Fire away,' I said, heading off one of the Coggs twins who was about to collide with me and capsize the tea.

'I've only just made up my mind,' said Mrs Bonny, looking singularly unhappy.

'What about?' I asked.

Ernest and Patrick were fighting on the ground, rolling over and over in the dust, legs and arms flailing. I don't mind a certain amount of good-natured scrapping, but on this occasion their clothes were suffering, and Ernest's head was dangerously near a sharp post. I left Mrs Bonny to part them.

When I returned, she was twirling the wedding ring even more violently.

'I must go,' she blurted out.

'Where?' I said, bewildered.

'To Bournemouth.'

I stared at her. For one moment I thought she had gone off her head. 'To Bournemouth? Now?'

Mrs Bonny took a grip on herself. 'No, no. I'm explaining things badly. I mean, I shall have to leave the school. I must give in my notice. Theo thinks it's best. We've talked it over.'

This was dreadful news. I looked at my watch. It was rather

early, but this must be discussed in the comparative peace of the classroom.

I blew the whistle, and we took the reluctant children into school.

'Now, tell me,' I begged, when we had settled the children to work, and she had come into my room, leaving the adjoining door open so that the infants could be under observation while we talked.

'It's my daughter, really,' explained Mrs Bonny. 'She's been pressing us for some time to go and live near them. She's got two young children, as you know, and another due at Christmas. I could help her a great deal, and I said that if she could find a suitable flat for us, we'd think about going.'

'Oh, Mrs Bonny,' I wailed, '*must* you go?'

The thought of finding another teacher filled me with despair. I have endured, in my time, a succession of temporary teachers, known as 'supply teachers', and though some have been delightful, more have been deplorable. Moreover, it is very unsettling for the children to have so many changes.

'I'm sorry it's such short notice,' said Mrs Bonny. 'I thought of leaving at the end of October – at half term. That would have given you plenty of time to find someone else. But this flat has turned up.'

I laughed hollowly. Finding a good infants' teacher is like searching for gold dust.

'And we should have had time to get the flat ready at weekends and during the summer holidays. But we've had a good offer for our house, and we feel we must sell it and go now.'

She seemed to have given the matter much thought, and obviously her mind was made up. I did my best to look at it from her point of view, but I felt sad and apprehensive.

A pellet of paper, obviously catapulted from a bent-back ruler, landed on my desk, and for a minute my staffing problems were forgotten.

Ernest, still holding the ruler, was scarlet in the face. 'I never meant –' he began fearfully, noting my expression.

'No play for you this afternoon,' I told him. 'You can write out your multiplication tables instead.'

Meekly, he picked up the pellet and put it in the waste-paper basket. At the same moment, a bevy of infants converged upon the communicating door, babbling incoherently.

Mrs Bonny and I went to see what was the matter. Beneath one of the diminutive armchairs a pool of water darkened the floorboards. The children pointed at one wispy five-year-old accusingly.

'Rosie Carter went to the lavatory,' said one self-righteous little girl.

'*That*,' said Mrs Bonny, with awful emphasis, 'is exactly what she did *not* do.'

We postponed our plans for the future to deal with more urgent problems.

15. SERGEANT BURNABY FALLS ILL

For some days after the departure of Mrs Fowler's dog, peace reigned at Tyler's Row.

Sergeant Burnaby maintained an offended silence when his path crossed the Hales'. Even his radio seemed quieter, although his cough, Diana noticed, became more hacking daily. She wished he would smoke less, but it was really none of her business, she told herself, and there were very few pleasures left for the old man to enjoy.

Mrs Fowler, too, seemed unusually quiet, and was inclined to toss her head and look the other way when Diana met her. It was a pity that she felt like this, thought Diana, but nothing could be done about it, and at least things were more tranquil.

She was glad of the respite, for she awaited the results of the tests with acute anxiety. She did her best to put aside her fears, busying herself with the house and garden, and with entertaining all those Caxley friends who wanted to see their new home, but now and again the grim doubts would break through her defences, and she would be beset by dark thoughts.

She felt sure that the wretched mole, which had started all the trouble, was growing. It was certainly giving her twinges. If only she could know! Even the worst news would be better than this torturing suspense.

It was during this waiting period that the Hales invited the Mawnes to dinner. Peter's headmaster, another keen ornithologist, and his wife, were also invited.

'Henry Mawne,' said Diana, as she set the table, 'reminds me of one of my old flames.'

'Which one?' asked Peter. 'That terrible tennis-player I met?'

'No, no. He didn't last long. D'you know, I can't for the life of me remember this man's name.'

Diana paused, forks in hand, and gazed into the middle distance. 'He had just been jilted by another girl called Diana, and he seemed to think it was the hand of God – meeting me, I mean. He was really rather persistent.'

'I expect you encouraged him,' said Peter primly.

'That I didn't! He was frightfully old, forty at least –'

'Poor devil!' commented Peter.

'And I was only twenty. He had a silver plate in his head, or a silver tube in his inside – something metallic one wouldn't expect – and such a nice voice.'

'What an incoherent description!' remarked Peter. 'I wouldn't trust your choice in an identity parade.'

'It's all I can remember,' protested Diana, resuming her work with the forks. 'Anyway, Henry Mawne is rather like him. How I wish I could remember his name!'

The headmaster and his wife arrived first. They were sticklers for punctuality, and if the invitation was for seven-thirty, they were there on the dot, if not a trifle earlier.

Diana, in common with most people, disliked visitors who kept one waiting whilst the meal grew browner and drier in the oven, but she sometimes wondered, when the Thornes appeared so promptly, if it were not harder to appear sincerely welcoming when one's back zip was still undone.

The Mawnes appeared at twenty to eight. Mrs Mawne, whom Diana had only seen in tweed suits or sensible cotton shirt-waisters, was resplendent in red velvet, cut very low, her substantial bosom supporting the sort of ornate necklace of gold, pearls and garnets, which Diana had only seen in the advertisements of Messrs Sotheby. She would really look more at home, thought Diana, at a gala performance at Covent Garden, rather than a modest dinner party in a cottage.

However, it was good of her to do the occasion so much honour, and she certainly looked magnificent. Henry, in his dark church suit, made a suitably restrained background to so much splendour.

The two men took to each other at once, and such terms as 'lesser spotted woodpeckers', 'only a *cedar* nesting box attracts them', 'migrator habits' and 'never more than one clutch a season', were batted between them like so many bright shuttlecocks.

The two women found that they had attended the same boarding school, and though they were both careful to make no mention of dates, thus giving away their ages, they remembered a great many girls and members of staff.

'And do you remember Friday lunch?' asked Mrs Thorne.

'Friday lunch,' said Mrs Mawne, with feeling, 'is permanently engraved – scarred, perhaps I should say – upon my memory. Those awful boiled cods at the end of each table, swimming in grey slime, with their poor eyes half out.'

'They might have looked better on a pretty dish,' said Mrs Thorne, trying to be fair. 'But those thick white dishes added to the general ghastliness.'

'At least you knew what you were eating,' said Diana. 'At

my school we had fish-cakes every Friday, concocted from sawdust and watered anchovy essence, as far as I could see. The irony of it was, they used to be dished up with a sprig of fresh parsley – the only thing with any food value in it at all – and, of course, that remained on the dish.'

'Have you noticed,' said Mrs Mawne, stroking her red velvet skirt, 'that everyone talks about food these days? I think we got into the way of it during the war, and now whenever women meet they swap recipes or reminiscences.'

'I know,' said Mrs Thorne. 'I remember my mother drumming into me as a child that a well-brought-up person never talked of politics, religion, money or food. We should all be struck dumb these days.'

Diana retreated to the kitchen to dish up. Mrs Willet was coming later to make the coffee, and to wash up when the meal was over. It was a long time since she had taken on such an engagement, and she had welcomed Diana's tentative invitation, with as much relish as if she were having an evening at the theatre. Diana hoped she would get a glimpse of Mrs Mawne's magnificence. It would please her so much.

The meal was a great success, the duck succulent, the fresh young vegetables, some from Mr Willet's garden, at their best, and Diana's strawberry shortcake sweet much admired.

Nothing, mercifully, could be heard of their neighbours. Ever since the earlier catastrophic dinner party when Robert was present, Diana had been painfully aware of how easily their peace could be shattered. The weather, perhaps, had something to do with it. The fine spell had broken, and heavy summer rain lashed the windows and dripped steadily from the thatch.

'Good for the grass,' commented the headmaster, who was a great gardener. The talk turned to flowers and trees, and then, suddenly, to neighbours.

'And how are you getting on with yours?' asked Mrs Mawne.

'Not very well,' confessed Peter, and told them a little of their troubles.

'You really must get rid of them,' Mrs Mawne maintained robustly. Diana hoped that Mrs Fowler's ear was not glued to the adjoining wall. Mrs Mawne's voice was notoriously carrying.

'That's easier said that done,' said Peter. 'They're sitting tenants.'

'I haven't seen the old soldier,' said Mr Mawne. 'At least, not since the weekend. Is he all right?'

'As far as I know,' said Diana. 'I think I saw him yesterday. Or was it the day before?'

'We often meet at the shop,' said Henry. 'I usually go to the Post Office at four, and he's going to buy his baccy. Interesting old fellow, but you don't want to be in a hurry. He'd talk till Kingdom Come if you'd let him.'

'He's lonely, I expect,' said Mrs Thorne. 'Particularly now, if he's taken umbrage about something, and isn't speaking to you.'

Diana began to feel worried. The conversation went on to other matters, but she had an uncomfortable feeling that it was quite two days since she had seen Sergeant Burnaby about. She must investigate as unobtrusively as possible. It was dreadful to think that the old soldier might be incapacitated so near at hand.

'I don't think we recognize', she heard the headmaster saying, 'how much the country lost when that generation was wiped out in the First World War. All the best, you know – the finest minds. Must make a difference to have all those potential fathers gone. I used to have *My Magazine* as a child. There were pages of photographs of some of the chaps who died. The Grenfell brothers, Raymond Asquith, Rupert Brooke, Charles Sorley and someone in a bush hat called Selous, as far as I remember. Just a handful of well-known men, of course. When you multiply that by hundreds, it makes you think of what we are still missing.'

'I had *My Magazine* too,' cried Diana. 'My parents thought I should learn such a lot from it. The first thing I did was to turn to "The Hippo Boys"! They once made a sledge out of an upturned table, and flew Union Jacks from all the legs.'

'A fat lot of education you seemed to have gleaned from *My Magazine*,' commented her husband. 'I don't think you picked up many of the pearls cast by the editors before all the young piglets. I had *Rainbow*, and was brought up on Mrs Bruin. I wonder why she had her frock decorated with a poached-egg pattern? It used to intrigue me.'

'Easy to draw, I expect,' said Henry Mawne. 'I wasn't allowed such luxuries, but I used to buy Sexton Blake in secret when I was at school, and read him under the bed clothes with a flickering torch.'

The party broke up about eleven. The rain still tumbled down. The Thornes had come from Caxley by car, but the Mawnes had come on foot, sheltering under golf umbrellas. By this time, there were formidable puddles everywhere, and despite protestations by Henry Mawne of enjoying a good splash through the rain – Mrs Mawne, for once, remaining silent – the Thornes insisted upon taking them home, and the Hales waved them all goodbye.

Diana looked anxiously towards Sergeant Burnaby's cottage. It was in complete darkness, as was Mrs Fowler's, but this was only to be expected at that time of night.

She found herself listening for sounds of life as she lay in bed an hour later. It was very quiet, and she made up her mind that she would call next door first thing in the morning, and risk the old man's wrath.

Then, faintly, she heard coughing. It was the old familiar rasping cough of the heavy smoker.

Much relieved, Diana turned over and fell asleep.

*

It was still raining the next morning when Peter went off to school. A long puddle, dimpled with raindrops, lay along the edge of the brick path, and the trunks of the trees were striped with little rivulets.

Still anxious, Diana peered through the hedge at Sergeant Burnaby's doorstep. She was shocked to see two full bottles of milk standing there in the rain. This must be the third day that the old man had been unable to go outside.

At that moment, the postman arrived. He called at the soldier's house first and then came to Diana's door. She enquired if he had seen Sergeant Burnaby.

'Come to think of it,' said the young man, dripping droplets from his peaked cap over the letters in his hand, 'I haven't. He's usually up and about. And now you mention it, yesterday's letter was still stuffed in his letter slit. You reckon he's okay?'

'I'm not sure,' replied Diana, 'but I'm going round immediately.'

'Shall I come too?'

'No, you've got your duties to do, many thanks. I'll manage. If need be, I can telephone for some help.'

The postman looked a trifle disappointed, Diana thought, at being denied a little drama, but she was sure that the fewer people who visited Sergeant Burnaby the better. No doubt she would get a hostile reception anyway, but she was willing to take the risk.

She shrugged on a mackintosh and splashed her way to the adjoining cottage.

The door was shut. She knocked and waited, watching the raindrops slide down the wood, and noting that all the windows were securely shut. After a minute or two, she tried the door handle.

The door was not locked or bolted, she was thankful to

find. She opened it a little way and called. There was no answer.

Now she began to feel afraid, and wished she had accepted the offer of the postman's company. Suppose the old man lay dead? The house was unnaturally quiet, and had the frowsty smell of an old house shut up for days without air.

She picked up the milk bottles. They rattled together in her shaking hand, and seemed to make a terrible din.

Taking a deep breath, she entered the living room. The fireplace had a few cold ashes in it. The windows were slightly misted with condensation. A crumpled newspaper lay on the floor by the old man's armchair. It was dated, Diana could see, three days earlier. Behind the door were more newspapers and two or three letters. She picked them up and put them on the table, still listening intently for any sound.

'Sergeant Burnaby!' she called at the foot of the stairs. There was no reply. She called again, louder now, her heart beginning to pound. Should she return and fetch help! No, she told herself, he might simply be sleeping soundly, and it was obviously sensible to find out first.

She mounted the stairs, calling as she went. Both doors at the head of the stairs were shut, but she knew that the old soldier's room was on the right-hand side, his wall adjoining their own house.

She rapped on the door, and stood listening, head on one side. There was no sound.

She rapped again, rather more loudly, and now there was the squeak of bed springs, and grunting noises.

'Can I come in?'

'Who's there?'

'Diana Hale. Are you all right?'

'What d'yer want?'

The voice was surly, but not unfriendly. Emboldened, Diana pushed open the door.

The old man's bristly face peered suspiciously over the bed

clothes. The room was stuffy, and the bed looked as though it had been used for two or three days without being made afresh.

'I was rather worried about you,' said Diana. 'We haven't seen you about and I wondered if you were ill.'

'I bin a bit rough,' admitted the old man. He looked thinner and his yellow face sagged. The fierce moustaches were down-bent, giving him an unusually depressed appearance.

'Let me get you a drink,' said Diana. 'What would you like? Hot milk, or tea, or something stronger?'

'I thought I had some tea,' said Sergeant Burnaby, looking about vaguely.

Diana took the empty cup from his bedside table. It was dry and stained, and had obviously been there for a day or two.

'I'll make you a fresh cup. When did you drink this?'

'Last night, I think. What's today?'

Diana told him. He looked disbelieving and slightly affronted.

'I come up here Monday night. Just after "Z Cars". Felt a bit rough with me chest.'

'I think you've been here ever since,' Diana said.

He put a hand to his ribs and winced. 'Got a sharpish pain here. Better sit up.'

She shook up the pillows and helped the old fellow upright. A spasm of coughing tore the man, and Diana was alarmed at the violence of the attack. She waited until it had passed and he leant back upon the pillows exhausted.

'I'll get your drink,' she said, 'and then I think we must get the doctor to have a look at you.'

'Don't want no damn doctor messin' me about,' wheezed the old man spasmodically.

Diana left him to make the tea. She could hear the sergeant's heavy breathing as she waited for the kettle to boil. She found a tin of biscuits and put them on the tray. There seemed to be remarkably little food in the pantry, but she did not like to pry too much. She resolved to bring him some home-made soup from home, and perhaps a boiled egg, if he could manage it.

He was grateful for the tea and drank it thirstily. Diana watched his trembling hands anxiously.

'Now, I'm going to pour you out a second cup, and while you drink it I'll ask the doctor to call on his rounds. Who do you have?'

'Young Barton at Springbourne. He's no good – like all of 'em. I tell you, I don't want nobody. I'll be all right if I rest.'

Diana said no more. She did not want to agitate him further, but she certainly intended to get help.

On her return to the cottage, she rang the surgery and was told that Dr Barton, though *excessively* busy, would call about twelve.

A little before midday, Diana went round again, bearing a light lunch. The old man was dozing, but woke at once and seemed almost pleased to see her.

She sat by the window and watched him eat. It would be best, she thought, to let him finish the meal before breaking the news of the doctor's impending visit. When he had finished, she brought him a bowl of warm water, soap and sponge, spreading the towel which hung from the bed rail across the old man's lap.

'That's better,' he said, mopping the drops from his chin. 'You bin a good neighbour to me this morning.'

He smiled upon her and Diana took courage.

'You may not think so when I tell you that Dr Barton's calling.'

'You ain't rung 'im?' protested Sergeant Burnaby, his face clouding.

'I had to,' replied Diana. 'You need an examination. It's the right thing to let your doctor have a look at you.'

'That's the worst of women,' said the old soldier viciously. 'Too damn interfering.'

He tugged crossly at the bedclothes, and was smitten with another racking attack of coughing. It was whilst this was in progress that the door opened and in walked the doctor.

Later, he came downstairs to where Diana was waiting.

'Are you a relative?'

'No, just a neighbour. The sergeant is our tenant.'

'He's pretty frail. Pleurisy and bronchitis, and his heart's not all it should be. What age is he?'

'Late seventies, I believe.'

The doctor nodded. 'Like most of these old people, he's underfed too. Can't be bothered to cook. All tea and biscuits. I'm sending the ambulance for him.'

Diana felt startled. She had not imagined that Sergeant Burnaby would need hospital treatment. The old man would be furious.

'Can you wait with him until it comes? I've several cases to attend to.'

'Of course.'

'Perhaps you could put a few things together for him? Pyjamas, soap – that sort of thing.'

He went out to his car, and Diana returned upstairs with some trepidation.

'Pleased with yerself?' asked Sergeant Burnaby nastily. 'Gets me out of the way, don't it?'

'Sergeant Burnaby!' protested Diana.

Something in her face must have touched the old soldier's heart. 'All right, all right! Don't start piping yer eye. I've got enough to put up with without that. Give us a hand with me clothes, gal. If I've gotter go to the blasted hospital, I'd better go decent.'

16. AMY'S PARTY

My friend Amy lives in the village of Bent, a few miles on the southern side of Caxley. I can take a roundabout route, through the lanes from Fairacre, and get there comfortably in half an hour.

The hedges were festooned with honeysuckle, the fragile trumpets giving out a wonderful scent in the warm evening air. Here and there, a late wild rose starred the greenery, and young fledglings squatted fearlessly among the grit in the road, and had to be warned of danger by a toot from the car's horn.

The corn was now golden, rustling in the light breeze which fanned the expanse, ruffling it like the wind across the sea. Soon the combines would be out, trundling round and round the acres like so many clumsy prehistoric beasts, while the farmers prayed for fine weather and freedom from mechanical breakdowns.

Nettled though I was by Amy's disparaging remarks about my perfectly good black dress, I had to admit that she had seen it a great many times, and perhaps a new one might be a good idea. Consequently, I was attired not in red but in an elegant affair of bottle-green, which I had bought at enormous expense in Caxley's leading stores. The hole which this extravagance had made in my monthly budget was truly horrifying. I comforted myself with the thought that it was an investment, and that I could probably live on eggs, which were plentiful and cheap, and the perpetual spinach which was rioting in my vegetable plot. If the worst came to the worst I should have to borrow some money from the needlework Oxo tin, as I had done before in times of financial stress.

Aunt Clara's seed pearls did nothing to enhance my ensemble, I had decided, and had dug out a fat silver brooch from Mexico which looked rather splendid, I thought, after a brisk rubbing with Silvo at the last minute. If I had been richer I should have bought a stunning pair of shoes to match my frock, but in the circumstances I polished my old black patent ones and was quite content.

How nice it is to grow old, I mused, as I trundled along between the hedges. Twenty years earlier, I should have worried about the shoes. Now I didn't care a tinker's cuss that they were old. I really would not care if I were going barefoot, except on Amy's account. There is a limit to eccentricity, even between old friends.

There were several cars in the drive when I arrived. I was glad I was not the first, as I am so often.

'It looks as though you never have a square meal,' Amy scolded once. 'Bursting in on the dot, and sniffing the air like a Bisto Kid!'

'I like to be punctual,' I had replied, with dignity.

Amy's house was built in the thirties, and has a prosperous

look about it with its wide eaves and pretty stonework. It looks across a valley, now golden with corn, towards distant hills to the south.

There were several people there whom I had met before and, surprisingly, the Mawnes from Fairacre. We greeted each other with unusual enthusiasm, meeting in a foreign part so unexpectedly.

'Let me present Mr Baker,' said Amy. 'Gerard Baker. Mrs Mawne and her husband, Henry Mawne. Miss Read. All from Fairacre, Gerard, and bursting with knowledge about Aloysius.'

I don't quite know what I had expected when Amy first told me about Gerard, but I was pleasantly surprised. Somehow, one does not expect a writer to look normal. If male, one half-expects a beard, or a mop of hair, or both, allied to a certain sallowness of complexion (burning midnight oil?) and either advanced emaciation because of failure to sell his work, or too much flesh because of unusual success.

Gerard Baker was neither thin nor fat, clean-shaven, with tidy fair hair and an air of cheerful competence. He would have made a reassuring dentist, or a reliable headmaster of a prep school.

All three of us explained hastily that we knew very little about the poet he was interested in, but I told him about Mr Willet's remarks, and he was eager to meet him.

'Aloysius sounds rather a trial,' he said. 'He's the sixth poet I've tackled so far, and to be frank, they are all proving to be hopeless domestically.'

'But surely it's their work you're considering,' said Mrs Mawne.

'Yes, but the men too. I've come to the conclusion that life with a poet – and the more minor the worse – must have been uncommonly depressing for his family.'

At this moment, Vanessa was brought up to meet the great man. She looked tidier than usual, but still pale and unhappy.

We drifted away as the movement of guests carried us, and let them converse.

Later, some of us wandered into the garden. Amy is splendidly up-to-the-minute with her garden. There are lots of shrubs and roses, and more foliage than flowers in her herbaceous border. As she is a keen flower-arranger, the place fairly bristles with hostas and dogwood, and lots of things with green flowers or catkins which are difficult to distinguish from the surrounding boskage.

A beautiful old lime tree scented the air, and I made a private bet with myself that not a branch entered Amy's house without being first denuded of its leaves. Did she still, I wondered, pop the young leaves against her mouth with a satisfying report? She had been a notable leaf-popper at college. Probably she had put such childish things behind her.

Whilst I mused, swinging my sherry in the glass, Gerard came to join me, and we went to sit on an elegant white wrought-iron seat which was much more comfortable than it looked.

'It's nice to be in the fresh air,' he confessed. 'Why do even the politest cocktail parties get so hot and noisy?'

I took this to be a rhetorical question and only smiled in reply.

'Do you know Vanessa well?' was his next question.

'Not very.'

'She seems such a charming child, but sad. Crossed in love I suppose. One always is at that age.'

I told him about the four times-married husband.

'But she looks better than she did,' I assured him. 'Amy tells me she's getting over it.'

'What a blessing it is to grow out of one's first youth,' said Gerard. 'Everything matters so terribly. So much to learn, so many mistakes to make. That line from "Gigi" – "Methuselah is my patron saint" – strikes a chord with me.'

'Me too,' I told him. 'I was thinking on much the same lines as I drove over here this evening.'

'Vanessa's staying here for a few days,' said Gerard. 'I wonder if she'd bring her aunt to lunch with me in Caxley? Do you think she'd find it boring?'

'Of course not. Ask her anyway. I'd say she'd be honoured.'

'Awful to be young,' he repeated, gazing across the valley. 'So vulnerable at that age – exposed to every blow, helpless, like a – like a –'

'Winkle without a shell?' I suggested, as he sought for words.

He threw back his head and roared with laughter. 'Exactly. I was searching for a much more poetic simile, but that hits the nail on the head.'

'We must go back and mingle,' I said. 'We've had our quota of fresh air.'

'I'll catch Amy now, before I go,' said Gerard, 'and ask about Vanessa.'

'Good luck,' I said, 'and if Amy can't come, I shouldn't let it worry you. After all, Vanessa is now legally an adult.'

As the guests drifted away, Amy took me to one side.

'Stop and help us eat up the bits, darling,' she begged, 'You won't have to wash up. Mrs Thingummy's come to help.'

'You misjudge me,' I said. 'I didn't think you wanted me to stay simply to do a bit of charring. And, yes please, I'd love to eat my way through those smoked salmon fripperies, not to mention the rolled asparagus tips.'

'It *is* useful to have a greedy friend,' exclaimed Amy.

Later, over enormous cups of coffee, Vanessa and I congratulated Amy on the success of the party.

'If only poor old James could have been here,' she said. 'He was called away this afternoon to some wretched meeting in Leicester.'

'Has he met Gerard Baker?'

'Yes, indeed. James introduced him to me. By the way, how did you get on?'

'Very well, I like his no-nonsense manner. He's not a bit as I imagined him.'

'He's invited Vanessa and me to lunch while he's in Caxley,' Amy said. 'Has he asked you, by any chance?'

'Alas, no. Any hopes you had of match-making, Amy, are in vain. Nice though he is, I doubt if Gerard is really interested in matrimony.'

Vanessa put down her cup with a crash, and sprang to her feet. 'How I do hate to hear people being picked over! I thought Mr Baker was the *kindest*, most *honest*, *sweetest* person I'd met for a long time. Not a bit like most grown-ups.'

She stalked to the door, slammed it behind her, and left us gazing at each other.

'Well!' I exclaimed.

Amy shrugged her shoulders and reached for another cigarette. 'The young', she said indulgently, 'are excessively trying.'

At Tyler's Row, Peter Hale was echoing Amy's thoughts. Before him stood a pile of school reports, for it was almost the end of term.

'Any news of the old chap next door?' asked Peter, pausing in his task.

'The hospital says he's comfortable,' replied Diana, looking up from her weekly letters to the boys.

'We all know what that means! Tubes stuck everywhere, a bed like rock, and being woken at five just when you've dropped off.'

'He's going to be there for a week or two,' she added. 'I'll go and see him one evening. I don't suppose he'll have many visitors.'

'What about things next door?'

'Mrs Willet's tidied up, and I've cancelled milk and papers and that sort of thing.'

'Not much more we can do then. It seems unnaturally quiet, doesn't it?'

Diana nodded. The windows were open, and only the sound of birds twittering, and a bee bumbling about the cotoneaster, could be heard.

Peter sighed. 'Well, can't sit here gossiping with these blasted reports waiting to be done. I often wonder what would happen if I put the literal truth. "The idlest boy I have ever met in over thirty years of teaching", for instance. Or "Is trying, in every sense of the word".'

'You would be assaulted and battered by enraged parents,' Diana told him.

'Or what about: "Needs a thorough caning for dumb insolence – and not always dumb".'

'Get on with them,' advised Diana, 'and keep those happy dreams to yourself.'

There was silence for a time while their pens worked steadily. Then Peter paused again.

'How's Mrs Fowler? She's remarkably quiet too. Is it because her old sparring partner's away?'

'Could be. She doesn't speak to me these days. But the dog's back, much to our Tom's annoyance.'

'Don't say he's starting a private war! I couldn't stand that.'

'Well, he goes through there quite often, and I should imagine he's sailing pretty near the wind. Mrs Fowler isn't above giving him a sly belting for trespass, particularly if he upsets her animal!'

'We must try and keep him in.'

'A cat? Impossible! He must just take his chance.'

They resumed their work, but Peter's mind wandered to other things. It was time Diana knew about the results of the doctor's tests. She had been wonderfully calm and cheerful during this waiting period, but if she were as worried as he was, then the suspense must be appalling. He could not bear to contemplate anything which would mar their happiness, or endanger Diana's health. Perhaps, he thought, they had been too lucky. Good health had always been theirs, and taken quite for granted. This shadow, which had fallen across them during the last few weeks, was something which a great many people lived under all their lives. It was a sobering thought.

'We must get away during the holidays,' he said suddenly.

Surprised, Diana looked up. 'But I thought we'd decided that it would be too expensive after the move? You know we've spent far more than we intended, and we've still got stage two of Bellamy's to face. That's bound to be even more crippling than stage one.'

'I know all that, but I still think we should get away for a few days. Somewhere not too far. We'll throw our stuff in the back of the car and push off to Wales or the Yorkshire Dales. Somewhere away from Tyler's Row and the confounded neighbours.'

'If you feel like that, we will,' said Diana. 'I'd love it, of course. We seem to have had so many niggling little worries since we came here. It *would* do us good to go and forget them, and come back quite fresh.'

'Right. Towards the end of August perhaps. Or early September.'

He picked up his pen again and attacked the next report.

'Now here's a boy who works well, plays hard, ought to go to University, and is going to leave now, at sixteen.'

'Why?'

'Dad says he wants him in the shop. We've talked to him until our lungs have collapsed, but he's a proper mule-headed individual, so that's that. There are dozens of others who ought to leave at sixteen and get their teeth into a job of work, and they're just the chaps that have besotted parents who imagine them as future dons.'

'That's life,' said Diana. 'No justice, is there? I think it's much easier to be happy if you recognize that from the start. People always seem to think that they should get what they deserve, and it so rarely works out that way.'

'Now that's a dangerous outlook,' commented Peter. 'Do you mean to say that no matter how you behave the results are predestined? In that case, why have any rules, or any code of ethics at all?'

'Not *quite* that,' began Diana slowly, when the telephone bell rang, and she was spared the task of elucidation.

'I'll go,' she said.

Peter heard her making monosyllabic replies, and hoped to goodness she was not agreeing to take on more duties than she could manage at the moment. People seemed to be forever ringing her up wanting gifts for bring-and-buy coffee mornings, or asking Diana to sell raffle tickets, or collect for flag days. Sometimes Peter felt like shooting these people who made such demands on his wife's time and energy. At the moment, particularly, he felt fiercely protective. He waited for her return, pen poised, but reports forgotten.

Diana appeared at the doorway. She looked perplexed and dazed. 'It was the doctor,' she said, and her voice trembled.

Peter's heart sank. He jumped to his feet, scattering the papers on the floor.

'He says everything's all right,' quavered Diana. 'No danger at all.'

Her face crumpled, and for the first time for years, Peter watched, with horror, his wife weeping.

17. SPECULATION IN FAIRACRE

That night Diana slept without waking, the first full night's rest for many weeks. She awoke to such a feeling of relief and joyousness that she sang as she dressed, and felt as impatient as a child to get on with the wonderful business of living.

Peter was equally relieved. 'Thank God, it's all over,' he said.

'Well, not quite. I can have this ugly thing taken off my neck at any time. It's only a tiny operation, and I'd be glad to have it done. I'll fix up an appointment in the holidays, I think.'

'Today,' said Peter firmly, 'we're lunching out to celebrate.'

'And this evening I'll pop in and see poor old Burnaby.'

'Better ring first,' advised Peter.

The hospital said that visiting hours were from seven to eight-thirty sharp, only two visitors at a time, and the side door only was to be used as the decorators were in, and Sergeant Burnaby was – as ever – comfortable.

'Welcoming lot,' commented Diana, as the receiver was replaced briskly at the other end before she had had time for further inquiries. 'I was going to ask if I could take him a bottle of something.'

'You take it,' said Peter. 'If there's any place you need a drop of the hard stuff, it's in a hospital bed.'

'You don't know anything about hospital beds! You've never been in one in your life.'

'I had my tonsils out at six, I'll have you know.'

'But no hard stuff in the locker then.'

'Well, no. But I had enough ice-cream to make an igloo. Absolutely delicious, except it hurt like hell to swallow anyway.'

'I shall take him some Burgundy,' Diana decided. 'And some Lucozade.'

'So that he can make a cocktail?' asked Peter, grimacing at the thought.

'In case he's not allowed to drink alcohol.'

'You shove it in his locker anyway. He'll find a use for it. No doubt the nurses could do with a glass. Make a change from nips of surgical spirit.'

'I'm quite sure', said Diana, 'that the staff of Caxley Cottage Hospital is above reproach. Nips of surgical spirit indeed!'

'You don't want me to come too?'

Peter looked apprehensive. He had a horror of hospitals, Diana knew. She felt she would sooner face the visit on her own, and said so. The relief on Peter's face made her laugh.

'You can go next time,' she teased him.

They drove for lunch to a riverside pub, where the swans and ducks scattered bright drops of water as they scurried to collect the largesse thrown to them by children on the green bank. The willows trailed in the current, and now and again a punt floated by, its occupants wearing that vague glassy-eyed expression of bliss, which moving water evokes. Nearby, a weir tossed its frothing waters in roaring cascades, in contrast to the quiet main stream.

For Diana, her senses sharpened by happiness and escape from months of tension, the scene was unforgettable. It was, she decided, one of the most perfect moments of her time with Peter.

The side door of Caxley Cottage Hospital led into a corridor redolent of floor polish and disinfectant. Diana, bearing her two bottles, followed the dozen or so visitors along the passage-way to a central hall which had a signpost standing in the centre.

She seemed to be the only one going to the Men's Ward, and she wondered, idiotically, if Sergeant Burnaby could be the sole inmate. The ward was not very large, probably less than twenty beds altogether, Diana guessed, at her first quick glance, and Sergeant Burnaby, propped upon snowy cushions which accentuated the habitual primrose hue of his face, was very close to the door.

He caught sight of her and smiled delightedly, but to Diana's dismay she saw that an elderly couple were sitting one each side of the bed. Mindful of the stern warning that only two visitors were allowed at a time, she began to retreat, but Sergeant Burnaby hailed her with all his usual vigour.

'Come on in, ma'am! Come on in!'

Diana did as she was told. 'I thought I'd better wait outside,' she said. 'Surely you are only allowed two visitors?'

'Lot of nonsense!' declared the old man. 'Don't take no notice of it. Nobody else does.'

He waved a hand round the ward, and certainly there seemed to be plenty of patients with a number of friends and relatives around them, nibbling grapes, distributing clean pyjamas, and admiring the banks of flowers.

'My old friends,' said Sergeant Burnaby, by way of introduction. 'My old comrade Jim Bennett and Alice his sister. I forgot, Jim, you didn't know this was the lady as bought Tyler's Row off of you.'

'And very nice it is,' said Diana. 'When are you coming back there?' she asked the patient.

'Can't get no sense out of 'em. Might be another two weeks or even longer. It's me chest, see. I'm fine otherwise.'

'He won't be long in here,' Jim Bennett assured Diana. 'He's a tough old bird.'

'Have to be,' commented Alice, 'to stand up to life in hospital.'

Diana took to this calm, fresh-faced countrywoman with her dry wit. She looked the sort of person who could cope with life perfectly, in hospital, or anywhere else.

'Have you had far to come?'

'Beech Green. There's a handy bus in.'

'I go through Beech Green – but, of course, you know,' said Diana. 'Would you like a lift back?'

'Very much indeed. There's only one bus back, and that's at nine-twenty. We're thinking of bed by then, Jim and me.'

'I've known old Jim,' remarked Sergeant Burnaby, struggling to sit upright, 'for nigh on sixty years. We've bin through

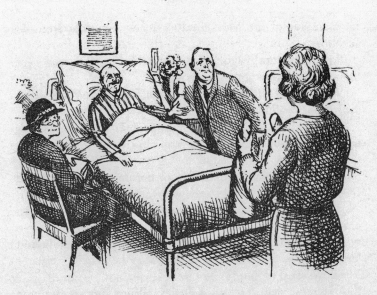

plenty together haven't us, eh? Remember that estaminet near Poperinghe?'

He began to chuckle at their private joke, and started a fit of coughing. It was so violent that Diana wondered if she should summon a nurse, but Alice Bennett propped pillows at his back, and offered some water, and the old man was quiet again in a minute.

'Have you been a nurse?' asked Diana, full of admiration for such competence.

'Done a bit with our parents. They was bedridden for several years, poor souls, but I haven't been trained. Wish I had. It's the life I'd have liked.'

'Tell us about the village,' wheezed Sergeant Burnaby. 'Any gossip? Any births, deaths or marriages? And what about that old faggot, Mrs Fowler? She dropped dead, yet?'

Diana did her best to make a diplomatic reply. She told him that Mrs Willet had tidied the cottage ready for his return, that their gardens were full of roses, and various other innocent topics, leaving out Mrs Fowler's name carefully from her account.

'Pity about me brass,' said the old man. 'I does it every Saturday. It'll be a real mess by now.'

'Mrs Willet will be pleased to do it I know,' said Diana swiftly. 'If you'll let her, that is.'

'May as well,' Sergeant Burnaby said. His tone was grudging. Clearly, he did not trust anyone to cherish his brass as he did himself.

A sister appeared, impressive in her dark blue and white. Diana felt guilty, as though she were a youthful wrong-doer.

'I think I'd better go, and leave you to talk for a little. I'll be in the car. There's no hurry.'

She put the two bottles on Sergeant Burnaby's bedside locker.

'Now, that's handsome of you, ma'am,' said Sergeant Burnaby. His moustaches seemed to tilt up another degree or two.

'Hope you enjoy it,' responded Diana. 'My husband may call in to see you if you have to stay some time.'

'Very welcome. Very welcome,' replied the old man.

Diana thought he was beginning to look tired, made her farewells, and walked rapidly from the ward before the sister took her name for detention.

It was very peaceful waiting in the car, and Diana thought how fascinating it was to sit there, virtually unseen, and watch people going about their affairs. A child, left in the next car whilst its parents were inside the hospital, was blissfully unaware of Diana, not six yards away, and was systematically licking the side window, her pink tongue working from top to bottom making wavering stripes of relative cleanliness.

An old man, cap set dead straight upon his ancient head and a camel-hair muffler making a neat V at his withered throat, was beating time incongruously, presumably to the music of a transistor set inside the car. How odd people were on their own, thought Diana, and wondered if she too was equally enthralling to some other unseen watcher nearby.

Jim and Alice Bennett soon emerged. Alice took a back seat, and Jim settled with a gratified sigh by Diana.

'How does he seem, do you think?' asked Diana.

'Not too good. We managed to get a word with the duty sister on our way out. They won't let him out until he has someone to take responsibility for him. Not fit to live alone again evidently.'

Diana had a brief vision of trying to look after the old soldier herself with the help of the district nurse. Could she possibly cope? For a week or two, no doubt. Permanently, it would be impossible.

'Any chance of an old people's home?'

'He'd hate that,' said Jim. 'No, Alice and I've talked this over in the last few days, and we don't see why he shouldn't come to us.'

'It's extremely generous of you,' said Diana, trying to keep the relief from her voice.

'No more'n he'd do for us. We've been through a lot together. I couldn't see him in want, and we've got a good spare room downstairs we can fit up for him with his own bits and pieces.'

'It's a lot for your sister to take on,' said Diana, stepping on the brakes. A short-skirted mother, giggling with a friend, had pushed her pram well out into the road without bothering to look either way, oblivious of the possible outcome to her helpless baby.

'Me?' Alice Bennett sounded surprised. 'Lor, I shan't mind! We can all get along together – three old folk can help each other a lot, and I've always been fond of the old boy. He won't be any trouble.'

She spoke with such calm cheerfulness, almost as though she welcomed the extra responsibility, that Diana felt ashamed of her own relief. How mean-spirited she was compared with this generous woman! Here was someone who really did love her neighbour as herself, and was happy to serve him, despite the fact that she herself was getting on in years, her house was small, and there could not be much money to spare.

She dropped the couple at Beech Green. It was beginning to get dark, and as she wound her way back to Fairacre along the shadowy lanes, Diana felt chastened by the difference in her own attitude to Sergeant Burnaby's future, compared with his old friends'.

Peter's reaction to the news was much more practical. 'Well, this brings stage two of Bellamy's plan a step nearer.'

'Do you know,' said Diana, 'I never thought of that.'

'Savour the situation now,' advised Peter. 'It's an ill wind that blows nobody any good.'

Rumours flew swiftly about Fairacre. Sergeant Burnaby's condition gave rise to considerable speculation, and the news that he would not be returning to Tyler's Row caused even more.

'Whatever the doctors say,' Mrs Willet told Diana, 'I reckon the poor old man's suffering from yellow jaundice. It's plain from his looks. My niece looked just the same some years ago, and Dr Martin had to come six or seven times to get her over it.'

'I don't think it's that,' ventured Diana. But Mrs Willet, busily polishing windows, was intent on her own theories.

'My sister knew what it was at once, and as soon as Dr Martin put his head in the door she told him. Proper cross, he was. He can be pretty sharp when he likes. "And how do you know?" he says to her, sarcastic. "It don't need much learning to see what she's got," my sister said. "She's yellow as a guinea." "I'll do my own diagnosing," he told her, and examined the child. "Well?" says my sister. "Yellow jaundice," he said, and was fair nettled when my sister laughed.'

At the meeting of the Women's Institute, held in the garden

of the vicarage, by kind permission of Mrs Partridge, Diana heard more theories put forward.

'Malaria,' boomed Mrs Pringle, resplendent in a navy blue straw hat decorated with a white duck's wing on the brim. 'It comes of visiting foreign parts. Mind you, Sergeant Burnaby was bound to go, being a soldier and under orders, but when I see the risks people run taking these holidays abroad among the foreigners and the germs and the water-not-fit-to-drink, I fairly trembles for them. And paying good money too to ruin their health!'

Mrs Mawne had heard, she told Diana over the teacups, that he was not expected to live. Pneumonia, wasn't it, and some virulent infection of the lungs? And what, if it wasn't being too premature, did the Hales propose to do about the cottage? If they were going to let it, until Mrs Fowler's became vacant too, she knew of a delightful couple, very musical, one with the flute and the other with the trumpet, who would make charming neighbours.

Mrs Johnson, hovering on the verge of the conversation, said that her husband knew of several young men, working with him at the atomic power station, who would be glad to rent a little place, no matter how primitive and inconvenient, until they could find better accommodation.

And the vicar too, amazingly enough, took Diana to admire his yellow roses, and in comparative privacy, away from the crowd of women, broached the subject of Sergeant Burnaby and his home.

'It sounds as though the poor fellow will be called to higher things before long,' he began, and before Diana could refute this statement, he continued.

'You may know that our infants' teacher at the village school has had to retire. Of course, the advertisement is in the *Teachers' World* and the *Times Educational Supplement*, and we hope to have a number of applicants. Accommodation is always such a problem for these young single women. In the old days, one could count on lodgings here and there, but there is *no one*, simply *no one*, who will board a girl in the village. Anyway, most of the young people seem to want to do for themselves, and Sergeant Burnaby's little place would be absolutely suitable, if you decide to let.'

'There is no question of it,' said Diana, with unaccustomed vigour. 'There is still a chance of the sergeant returning. As far as I know, he will be discharged from hospital in the next week or two. Friends are going to offer to have him with them, I believe, but he is an independent old man, as you know, and if he wants to return, then of course he must. In any case, at some time in the future we hope to incorporate the two end cottages into our own house.'

The vicar looked crestfallen. 'Quite, quite! I felt I must mention the matter to you, as we shall be holding our interviews before long, and a little cottage, such as yours, would be an added attraction to the post.'

Two more people approached Diana before the meeting ended to inquire about Sergeant Burnaby and to broach the subject of renting his cottage. Diana began to feel hunted, and was relieved when she could get away, and walk through the village to Tyler's Row.

On her way, she called at the Post Office. A woman, whom she had not seen before, was chattering to Mr Lamb.

'Poor old soul,' she was saying, 'and to think those new folk have driven him out of his own home! Want to add it to their own, I hear. Can you believe it? The way some people –'

Mr Lamb, getting rosier in the face every second, broke in upon the torrent of words. 'This is the lady who lives at Tyler's Row now, Mrs Strong.'

The woman had the grace to look abashed, but her ready tongue continued its work.

'We lived there for a time as children, me and my brothers. I was talking over old times with Mr Lamb here.'

Diana nodded, not trusting herself to speak.

'Well, I must be off. Takes a good twenty minutes over the hill to Springbourne.'

Mr Lamb and Diana watched her depart in silence. It was plain to the postmaster that Diana had heard every word. He spoke comfortingly.

'I shouldn't take any notice of what Effie Strong says, ma'am. She's got a tongue as reaches from here to Caxley.'

'I only hope that other people aren't thinking as she is. My husband and I are fond of Sergeant Burnaby, and hope he will soon be fit enough to come home. You may tell anyone this who is spreading such dreadful rumours.'

'There won't be any need,' Mr Lamb assured her. 'Fairacre's a shockin' place for gossip, but in their hearts people know the truth.'

And with this crumb of comfort, Diana had to be content.

Peter's comments were much the same.

'Let 'em tittle-tattle. We know we've nothing to reproach ourselves about. Dammit, the old boy might have snuffed it, if you hadn't gone to the rescue! If he's pining to come back and can manage on his own again, then he must have the place, of course.'

He paused to sneeze, fifteen times in quick succession.

'Those blasted pinks!' he gasped. 'But let's hope,' he continued, 'that Fate protects us from him after all.'

Honesty was one of Peter Hale's strongest virtues.

18. END OF TERM

Fairacre School said goodbye to Mrs Bonny with genuine regret.

The last few days of term had been over-shadowed by the problem of what to buy for her leaving present. All negotiations had to be conducted in secrecy, and many a sibilant whispering in my ear had driven me close to hysterics-by-tickling.

Ernest had suggested a silver tea-service. Someone had received such a gift after fifty years in the Caxley Borough offices, and no doubt the photograph in the *Caxley Chronicle* inspired Ernest's suggestion. When I pointed out the probable price, it was generally agreed that such richness was beyond our resources.

Joseph Coggs nobly offered a pair of rabbits, as his doe had just had a litter of eight, and was willing to make a hutch to house them if he could get a wooden box from the stores. I was much touched by this generous offer, but felt that Mrs Bonny might find it embarrassing. Joseph and I discussed the matter solemnly, and he agreed that transporting them would be exceedingly difficult, and that the sea air might not agree with country-bred rabbits. Regretfully, the children turned down Joseph's suggestion, though there were plenty of offers to have any surplus rabbits for themselves, if Joseph wanted homes.

The girls' suggestions were rather uninspired, running to such things as scent, handkerchiefs and boxes of chocolates. The boys were outspokenly scornful.

'Has them for Christmas!'

'Scent! Proper soppy!'

'She don't eat chocolate. I know, 'cos she didn't want a bite off my Mars Bar Thursday.'

'We wants to give her summat that'll last,' said Patrick. 'Like a tray.'

This inspired suggestion was greeted in respectful silence. It was Joseph Coggs who broke it.

'A tray'd be just right. We could get a little 'un for by her bed, or a big 'un for carrying out the washing up.'

I thought Patrick's idea was quite the best we had heard, and promised to go shopping in Caxley on Saturday on their behalf.

'Two-eighty us 'as got,' Ernest impressed upon me. 'Should

get a good 'un for that. I suppose if you saw a real smasher for three pounds us might put a bit more towards it.'

I said I would be happy to add a little extra but Ernest, brought up in a strict evangelical home, would have none of it.

'No, no! That's not right. You got enough to do with your money. It's the school's present, this is.'

Has he, I wondered, ever seen me rifling the Oxo tin when hard pressed? In any case, I admired his honourable outlook, and said I would do my best with the resources available.

That settled, we were able to cope with end-of-term activities such as Sports Day – refreshment tent under the kind super-vision of the Parent–Teacher Association – clearing out cup-boards, dismantling the nature table, writing reports, checking stock and so on.

Mrs Bonny was delighted, on the last afternoon, with her present of a sturdy carved oak tray, responded charmingly to the vicar's little speech, and invited us all to visit her whenever we were in her area.

Fairacre School broke up in a clamour of well-wishing, and the children streamed down the lane, shouting with exhilaration at the prospect of almost seven weeks of freedom.

Those mothers who had come to collect their offspring looked rather less joyous, I noticed.

One morning, in the early part of the holidays, I was wander-ing happily round the garden enjoying the morning sunshine. There is something wonderful about being free and outdoors at ten o'clock in the morning, when normally one is facing decimals or life in Anglo-Saxon England.

I was admiring my sweet williams and trying to persuade myself that they would do another year without splitting them when a car drew up, and out leapt Gerard Baker.

The passenger's door opened and, to my surprise, Vanessa emerged. She was actually smiling.

'Hello,' shouted Gerard. 'I'm Aloysius-hunting.'

'Well, he's not here,' I told him, 'but how lovely to see you both. Come and sit in the sun.'

'I came along for the ride,' said Vanessa, by way of explanation. 'Gerard brought Aunt Amy a book this morning, and offered me a lift. I feel rather a fraud. I'm sure I should never be able to do research on anything at all.'

She looked with open admiration at Gerard. This was the longest speech I had ever heard Vanessa utter. Gerard Baker certainly seemed to work miracles.

'Rubbish!' said Gerard. 'You've a very good brain. I'm going to ask you to make notes on this morning's discoveries. I'm sure you'll do it beautifully.'

He spoke briskly, like a kindly schoolmaster to a dim but striving pupil. I had to admit that the treatment seemed to be working.

'We've really called for directions. Can you tell us where Tyler's Row is? And do you think the people there will let us look at the cottage?'

I told him about Sergeant Burnaby's illness, and about the Hales who would be next door.

'But you simply must visit Mr Willet in the village before you go,' I said. 'He's the real authority on Loyshus. He had to sit through hours of his poem-readings. A real case of "And did you once see Shelley plain?"'

'Does Shelley come into it?' asked Vanessa.

'A quotation,' explained Gerard. 'Shelley lived some time before Aloysius.'

'And wrote rather better poetry,' I added. 'Have some coffee.'

'Now, that's *real* poetry,' raid Gerard. 'I didn't have breakfast this morning.'

'Why ever not?' demanded Vanessa, looking protective. 'It's very wrong to miss breakfast. It sets you up for the day, and burns up all sorts of toxic whatnots.'

'You', I said accusingly, 'have been listening to Aunt Amy. I bet she's on another dieting bout.'

'She is.'

They followed me into the kitchen, Gerard giving little grunts of appreciation as he came.

'This Victorian Gothic period is really due for a come-back. The windows of your school are perfect, and I love that pointed doorway.'

'Draughty,' I told him.

'And this house! A perfect period piece. What lovely wide window-sills!'

'I had those put in ten years ago.'

Gerard was unabashed, and peered round the kitchen door interestedly.

'Oh, but you've modernized this! What a pity!'

'The Beatrice stove wore out,' I said, 'and the kitchen range needed to be burnished daily with emery paper, and black-leaded as well. Life wasn't long enough. Filling oil lamps and trimming wicks took more time than I could spare, too.'

'Yes, I suppose so. No doubt, electricity does make things simpler.' But he sounded disappointed nevertheless.

Over coffee, Vanessa told us that she was hoping to get a post at an hotel in Scotland in the early autumn.

'More fun than an office, and I can use my typing and bookkeeping, as well as meeting lots of people, and helping to look after them. Meanwhile, Aunt Amy says I can stay at Bent as long as I like, or I can go home. I feel terribly lazy, but better in health since I've been here.'

And in spirits, was my unspoken comment. Clearly, the middle-aged philanderer was fast being forgotten.

'You just want to find as many interests as possible,' advised Gerard, 'until you get snapped up in matrimony in about six months' time.'

Vanessa turned great soulful eyes upon him.

'I shall never marry,' she told him earnestly. 'Never.'

'Don't you believe it,' was the robust reply. 'If you aren't the adored wife of some nice young man, with a baby in a pram on the lawn, within two years, I'll eat my new Irish tweed deer-stalker.'

Vanessa shook her dark head sadly.

'Come on, my dear,' said Gerard, jumping up. 'Work to do. The notebook's waiting for you in the car, and we must be off to Tyler's Row and Mr Willet.'

'Good luck with Loyshus!' I called after them, as they proceeded, with a series of alarming reports from the exhaust.

A day or two later, I met Mr Willet as I went to buy my groceries.

'Very nice couple you sent me,' he said, leaning over his gate. 'They thinking of gettin' wed?'

'I shouldn't think so.'

'Ah well! Might be a case of May and December, though he's a *clever* man there's no denying.'

'I'm sure you were able to tell him quite a lot about Aloysius.'

'A tidy bit. He wanted to know what he looked like. "Proper mess," I told him. "Gravy stains all down 'is front, and none too fragrant behind the ears." 'E never 'ad a bath, you know, Miss Read, not for months and months towards the end.'

'He might have done if he'd had a bathroom.'

'A bathroom!' echoed Mr Willet, with scorn. 'None of us had no bathrooms, but we all kep' clean. We heaved the old tub in afore the kitchen fire of a Saturday night, and got out the scrubbing brush, and a chunk of yellow soap chopped off of the bar with the coal shovel, and we fair went to town. But not ol' Loyshus, not him!'

'Did Mr Baker see his cottage, do you know?'

'Yes, Mrs Hale took him in herself. That gal of his took a shine to it. Said she'd like to live there herself.'

'I wonder.'

'Tell you what, though,' said Mr Willet, lowering his voice. 'That Mr Baker don't know a thing about gardening. I was takin' him round the vegetables, and he never knew peas from carrots. What's more, when I was talking about my Kelvedon Wonder he kept looking across at my border and saying: "Which flowers are they?" It shook me, I can tell you. Been to school, and college too, I hear, and don't recognize Kelvedon Wonder. Makes you think about raisin' the school leavin' age, don't it? I mean, if a boy don't know about Kelvedon Wonder by fifteen, when's he going to?'

I thought the subject should be changed swiftly, as I was not too sure about Kelvedon Wonder myself, and asked him to come and have a look at the school skylight some time before term started.

'I'll do that,' he assured me, 'though you knows as well as I do that that damn skylight's let water in for nigh on a hundred years, and ain't likely to stop now, unless we takes the bull by the horns one day and boards it over. That'd settle it!'

His eye brightened at the thought of vanquishing his old enemy, and I left him to his dreams.

Diana Hale was weeding the herbaceous border which ran down the garden, against the hedge which divided Mrs Fowler's garden from her own. On the whole, it had recovered very well from the onslaught of Mr Roberts' cows, and certainly the front of the border flourished.

But Diana was puzzled about the plants at the back. The tall delphiniums and lupins, the red-hot pokers and lofty Michaelmas daisies were looking decidedly peaky, and the leaves were turning brown. No doubt, Diana told herself, the old hawthorn hedge which had been there for so many years was the culprit, taking nourishment from the soil to the detriment of the newcomers. Nevertheless, it was perplexing.

As she pondered on the problem, Tom strolled through from Mrs Fowler's garden. Mrs Fowler appeared too, looking grim. Diana thought it might be a propitious time for extending the olive branch, and greeted her cheerfully.

'Lovely morning, Mrs Fowler. Are you well?'

'Mustn't grumble, I suppose,' said she, doing just that, from her tone.

'I do apologize for Tom. I hope he's not a nuisance to you. It's so difficult keeping a cat on his own premises.'

'Those of us with dogs has to,' commented Mrs Fowler tartly, 'or they gets criticized.'

She whisked indoors, and Diana resumed her weeding, very conscious that her olive branch had been thrown in her face.

Some days later. Tom was sick.

'What's he had for breakfast?' asked Peter, holding the shovel, a look of intense distaste on his face.

'Some new stuff, Pussi-luvs.'

'Well, ours doesn't obviously. I should throw the tin away. We don't get this trouble very often, thank God. The old boy's got a digestion like an ostrich's.'

A few days after this, Tom was sick again, and Diana was perturbed.

'Shall we get the vet?'

'No, don't bother him. He's obviously all right as soon as the stuff's out of the poor old chap. Has he had that rubbish again?'

'Pussi-luvs? No, just a morsel of liver this morning. He likes that normally.'

Tom's spirits certainly recovered quickly after the mishap, and nothing more occurred in the day or two before the Hales were due to set off on their brief holiday.

Kitty, their former neighbour in Caxley, was having Tom for the duration. He and Charlie could renew their friendship and their suburban hunting together.

Diana told Kitty about the mysterious attacks, but Kitty was reassuring.

'I'll watch his diet, don't worry. He probably picked up some mouse or shrew that had been sprayed with an insecticide – something of that nature. You two go off and enjoy your break. Tom will be happy enough here.'

Diana was unusually silent as they drove back to Tyler's Row. Kitty's remark about picking up something poisonous had started an alarming train of thought. Those flowers against the dividing hedge, the implacable malice with which her greetings were returned, could they really be clues to something sinister which was going on? Could anyone, even someone so spiteful as Mrs Fowler obviously was, set out to hurt an unsuspecting animal, simply because it trespassed?

Diana told herself the whole idea was far-fetched, and said nothing about her fears to Peter. Tomorrow they would be off on their travels, and heaven alone knew they both needed a rest. She welcomed the thought of leaving Tyler's Row and its troubles for a few days. What a relief it would be!

Nevertheless, the doubts remained at the back of her mind, and she wondered what the future might hold on their return.

19. THE LAST BATTLE

The Hales returned much refreshed from their few days' break. They had headed north, explored the Yorkshire Dales, and visited some of the fine towns for the first time. Richmond, in particular, delighted them, and they promised themselves a return trip one day.

It was a golden August evening as they drove down the slope of the hills which sheltered Fairacre. Already some of the fields had been harvested, neat bales of straw standing among the bright stubble, waiting to be collected.

Dahlias were out in the cottage gardens, and some tall chrysanthemums, their heads shrouded in paper bags, re-minded passers-by of the Caxley Chrysanthemum Show to come before long.

'It looks autumnal already,' sighed Diana. 'I wonder how our garden's looking?'

'Grass up to our hocks, I expect,' replied Peter. 'It always grows twice as fast if you go away.'

They turned into the garage, and surveyed Tyler's Row with satisfaction. The thatch glowed warmly in the rays of the sinking sun. Sergeant Burnaby's yellow rose was in full flower for the second time, and the scent of mignonette and jasmine filled the garden.

'We've seen some heavenly places,' said Diana, walking up the path, 'but this beats the lot.'

' "Every prospect pleases",' quoted Peter, 'and only the neighbours are vile.'

'Which reminds me,' said Diana. 'I must find out about Sergeant Burnaby's plans.'

They spent the next hour or so unpacking, eating poached eggs on toast, and ringing Kitty to let her know they were back.

'By the way,' Kitty said, 'Tom's in great heart. No sickness, enormous appetite, polite to Charlie – in fact, the perfect guest. Leave him here any time you want to.'

They arranged to fetch him the next day, and Diana took a final walk round the garden before it grew too dark to see.

The plants at the back of the border looked as unhealthy as ever. What could cause their malaise? Could Mrs Fowler really be attacking them? Surely no one would be so childish, thought Diana.

She looked towards her neighbour's cottage, and was amazed to see that two large white shells, which had once stood on each side of Sergeant Burnaby's doorstep, now flanked Mrs Fowler's. Above them, swinging from the thatch, was a hanging basket which the old soldier had kept filled with scraps for the birds.

Nonplussed, Diana went to the other hedge to check that Sergeant Burnaby's possessions had been moved. As she had suspected, the shells and basket had gone and, even more alarming, a number of holes in the garden gave evidence of plants having been dug up. No doubt, those too had found a home on Mrs Fowler's side of the hedge.

Diana told Peter about these matters as they prepared for bed.

'I had my suspicions about our border before we went away. This seems to prove that she is quite unscrupulous.'

'We'll go and have a good look round in daylight tomorrow,' said Peter, 'and that old besom is going to be faced with this. It's the last straw.'

'She'll think we want to turn her out so that we can get on with the conversion,' said Diana, remembering the conversation she had overheard in the Post Office.

'She knows perfectly well we can't give her notice to quit, but she's a constant menace. We've stood enough. This pilfering and damage is going too far.'

After breakfast, the next morning, Diana and Peter took the key, and inspected the premises next door. Mrs Willet had done a thorough job of cleaning and tidying. Sergeant Burnaby would have approved. The precious odds and ends of brass shone like gold, the leaded panes gleamed, and only the faintest hint of dust lay across the polished surfaces of the old man's furniture.

Diana stood still and looked about her. As far as she could see, nothing in here had been taken. Mrs Fowler had not been able to gain an entry obviously. The first things to have gone would have been the brass ornaments, Diana felt sure. Human magpie that she was, Mrs Fowler would have been unable to resist them.

They went upstairs, and all looked exactly as Diana remembered it. The old man's counterpane was neatly spread, a pair of shoes stood side by side on the thin mat beside the bed. There was water in the flowered ewer standing in its matching basin on the old-fashioned washstand. It all looked so expectant, thought Diana, awaiting the master of the house. Would he ever come back to bring these things to life again? The whole house was forlorn in its silence, and she longed for voices, music, a fire, a kettle singing, even a fly buzzing against the window – anything to chase away the pathetic stillness of the waiting rooms.

'Nothing seems to be missing.' she said at last. They returned to the garden, locking the door behind them.

The old man's weather beaten wooden armchair still stood beneath the thatch by the back door, but something had gone. Diana wrinkled her brow with concentration.

'That rustic table,' said Peter. 'Used to stand here for his pipe and baccy, and his glass of beer.'

Diana nodded. 'And the antlers,' she added. These had been

fastened to the wall. Bleached bone-white by years of Fairacre weather they had given no pleasure to Diana's eye, but had obviously been treasured by the old soldier. The shield-shaped mount had left a clear mark on the brickwork.

By daylight, they could see even more. Tell-tale holes where plants had been removed were numerous. It was difficult to remember the garden in detail, but they had seen enough to know that a marauder had been at work. Now all that was needed was to trace the stolen goods to Mrs Fowler's.

'We'll go round straight away,' said Peter, making for the gate.

'Wouldn't it be better if I called first?' said Diana, dreading a scene.

'*Straight away*,' repeated Peter, in a voice which brooked no argument.

Fearfully, Diana followed him as he strode towards Mrs Fowler's.

As so often happens, when one is girded for the fray, the enemy was not forthcoming. Mrs Fowler's cottage was as empty as Sergeant Burnaby's. Even the dog was absent.

They stood on the lady's doorstep and looked about them. The white shells gleamed from each side of the step. The rustic table was by the hedge, bearing a stone squirrel upon it. Several newly-planted clumps of flowers were apparent in Mrs Fowler's border, and a shallow slate sink, which Diana now remembered seeing in the old soldier's garden, stood by the house wall, strategically placed to catch any rain which ran down from the thatch, and so provide a bath for the birds. Beyond it, propped against the wall, were the antlers, awaiting their allotted place.

Here was evidence enough; the only thing missing was the accused.

'Blast!' said Peter. 'I was raring for a fight. Where d'you think she's gone?'

'Caxley,' said Diana. 'I've just remembered, it's market day. Let's go and fetch Tom, while our tempers cool.'

As one might expect, Tom was not present at Kitty's when the Hales arrived. After eating his own and then Charlie's breakfast, he had made off into a distant garden.

'I'll bring him over when he appears,' promised Kitty, and went to brew coffee. Just as they were about to go, the Hales saw Tom reappearing through the hedge, and Diana ran towards him with a cry of pleasure. Tom glared stonily at her. He was not going to be placated so easily. Besides, he had seen that confounded cat basket by the car.

He turned to escape, but Peter was too quick for him. Defeated, Tom allowed himself to be placed in the hated basket where he set up a dreadful banshee wailing which he managed to sustain all the way to Fairacre.

'He certainly looks magnificent,' said Diana, when at last he was released, and was stalking about the house inspecting things. 'I wonder what upset him before we went away?'

'Too much grub,' said Peter, dismissing the subject. Diana could see that he was alert for any small sound next door which might mean that Mrs Fowler had returned, and that he could engage the enemy.

But it was many hours later when their neighbour came home. Peter and Diana had gone to bed early, and it must have been midnight when they heard the familiar clatter of Mrs Fowler's nephew's van outside in the lane.

The door of the van clanged, farewells were shouted, the van chugged away, and the sound of Mrs Fowler's footsteps could be heard on the brick path. Snuffling and whining betokened the presence of the dog.

Suddenly, the whining changed to furious barking, and the enraged squawking and spitting of Tom. The two old foes had met again.

'So *you're* back, are you?' they heard Mrs Fowler say ominously. 'We'll have to see about you, my boy.'

Her door slammed, and silence once more enveloped Tyler's Row.

The next day, much to Peter's annoyance, he was called into school unexpectedly by the headmaster. Two members of staff, newly-appointed, were unable to start after the holidays, and this threw the time-table into unbelievable tangles. His visit to Mrs Fowler had to be postponed until the evening, and once again, she was out.

'Her niece and nephew fetched her in the van,' said Diana. 'They seem unusually attentive at the moment.'

Peter contented himself with mowing the grass while Diana set off to visit Sergeant Burnaby, who was still in Caxley Cottage Hospital.

As she approached the hospital, she overtook Jim and Alice Bennett walking up the hill from the bus station, and stopped to give them a lift.

'He's doing fine,' said Jim, replying to Diana's inquiries. 'They're letting him out next Wednesday. We've got his room ready. We went over to the cottage to collect some of his clothes while you were away.'

'It all looked very spick and span,' said Alice. 'Mrs Willet's got a good hand with housework. We're going to see what he wants in the way of his furniture. Jim's mate at the local said he'd fetch anything in the van.'

'Won't he want to come back himself to sort things out?'

'No. He's dead against it. It's that Mrs Fowler he can't stick. It's my belief, Mrs Hale, that he wouldn't go back there even if he was fit. She's poisoned Tyler's Row for the poor old chap – that she has!'

And not only for the poor old chap, thought Diana, drawing into the car park.

'Well, all I can say is Sergeant Burnaby's a lucky man to have such good friends,' said Diana.

'He's welcome,' replied Jim Bennett simply. The two words summed up the situation perfectly, thought Diana.

They found the old soldier sitting on a chair beside his bed, looking very much stronger and with a complexion faintly tinged with pink, for the first time in Diana's experience.

He was obviously excited at the thought of his new abode, and was full of plans.

'And what can I pack for you from the cottage?' offered Diana.

'I don't want much, Jim's fetched me clothes, and I'd better have me own china and eating irons. And me bits of brass! Must have them, and Jim says I can put me old chair in the garden in his arbour, so that'll have to come aboard.'

'Anything else?'

The old man ruminated. 'Them old shells by the door. I'd like them. Got 'em in India. They come off of some island in the Indian Ocean. I'm partial to them.'

'You shall have them,' promised Diana, determined to wrest them from Mrs Fowler by sheer force, if need be.

'Are you sure you don't want to have a look round for yourself?' she continued. 'We could fetch you one afternoon.'

The old man's expression grew mutinous. 'Not while that ol' cat's there. She curdles me. I feels the bile rising when I see her vinegar-face over the hedge. I don't want to see Tyler's Row again while she poisons the air.' He looked up at Diana sharply. 'She pinched much? Out of the house?'

'Nothing from the house. It was securely locked.'

Luckily, Jim put a question at this point, and Diana was spared the embarrassment of further examination by Sergeant Burnaby.

It was good to see him so forward-looking. Obviously, he was leaving Tyler's Row with relief, which made things easier for the Hales. Diana left the three to make their plans for the next Wednesday and waited, as before, to give the couple a lift back to Beech Green.

It was beginning to get dark as she drove into her garage, and the lights were on in the house.

Peter met her at the door, looking worried.

'Better get the car out again. Tom's pretty ill. The vet says he'll see him immediately if we take him in.'

They put the comatose cat into his basket. Tom was too weak to make his usual demurs, but occasionally gave a little whine of complaint which wrung Diana's heart.

The vet held Tom on the table. The cat's back arched and he was horribly sick. The vet studied the mess with an expert eye, examined Tom briefly, and spoke. 'He's been poisoned,' he said.

'Will he die?' cried Diana.

'No. He's practically cured himself by rejecting this lot, but I'll make sure with an injection.'

He went to work, and within ten minutes Tom was back in the car, and heading for home and convalescence.

'You know who's responsible?' Peter's tone was savage.

'I have my suspicions.'

'That woman', said Peter, 'doesn't know what's coming to her.'

It was, perhaps, fortunate for all concerned that Mrs Fowler's cottage was in darkness when the Hales returned. Once again, they were in bed when their neighbour returned in the ram-shackle van. Muttering vengeance, Peter tossed in his bed as he heard the lady enter her home.

At eight-thirty the next morning he strode next door. Diana's presence, he told her, was not necessary.

'I'll do a better job alone,' he told her. 'You'll be too soft-hearted. I'm threatening the old hag with the police, and if she pipes her eye, all the better. If you're there you'll let her off with an invitation to tea.'

Diana watched him go with mixed feelings. She was relieved to be spared the encounter, but apprehensive about Peter's force. He had been so furious about poor Tom, he might even strike Mrs Fowler. The thought led Diana immediately to a court scene, with Peter in the dock facing a row of ferocious-looking magistrates, all bent on sending him forward to Assizes or Quarter Sessions or Crown Court, or whatever its new-fangled name was, with a recommendation for deportation, probably in iron gyves like Eugene Aram.

Diana contemplated this flight of fancy for some minutes, and then carried the breakfast things to the sink, and returned to earth.

It was ominously quiet next door – no raised voices, no crashing of china, no heavy thuds of close-in fighting. Perhaps Peter had felled her with one blow as she opened the door? How long, Diana wondered, coffee pot in hand, did one get for Grievous Bodily Harm? She began her washing-up, ears strained to hear any significant sound through the wall.

There, standing facing each other across the table, were the two adversaries. A fine geranium in a pot stood centrally upon a plastic tablecloth which was decorated hideously with im-probable scarlet flowers upon a sky-blue trellis work. Peter refused to let this monstrosity distract him from the task in hand. He spoke sternly.

'I've come about a serious matter. Can you tell me why Sergeant Burnaby's property is now on your premises?'

'Such as?' queried Mrs Fowler, with cool insolence.

'The two ornamental shells, the antlers, that little table by the hedge, the bird basket, and – I strongly suspect – a great many of the new plants in your garden there.'

'It so happens,' said Mrs Fowler, 'that I bought those odds and ends in here for safe keeping, until the old man got back from hospital. You should know there's thieves in Fairacre. You had plenty took afore you moved in.'

'And the plants?'

'Who said I took any plants?' She leant across the table menacingly. 'You comes in here, accusing me. Well, prove it.'

There was certainly plenty of fight in Peter's enemy. She was going to be a tougher nut to crack than he had first thought.

'You can tell what tale you like,' he told her. 'Frankly, I don't believe any of it. This could be a case for police investigation, you know.'

'Police!' Mrs Fowler spat out the word. 'I know your sort. You've been angling to get me and the sergeant out of Tyler's Row ever since you set eyes on it. Well, you've got your way with the old boy. Now it's my turn, I suppose. Let me tell you, Mr Toffee-nose, I'll go when it suits me. You can't turn me out.'

Peter, ignoring this bitter truth, continued steadily. 'There are other matters, too. I suspect that you have been doing your best to poison the plants in our border, and have made some attempt to do the same to our cat.'

'What that cat picks up when he's trespassing's no business of mine. You should keep him home, like I have to do my dog.'

'There's such an offence as malicious damage, as well as stealing,' warned Peter. 'Now, you understand, this sort of thing just won't be tolerated. You will have to change your ways if we are to remain neighbours.'

'You can keep your threats,' sneered Mrs Fowler. Her eyes were glittering strangely. A red flush had crept up her withered neck into her face. She came round the table, and Peter half-expected a blow in the face.

'Listen here, you. I know when I'm not wanted. I'm giving *you* notice. I wouldn't stay in this place another winter, if you paid me to. I've made me plans already, and I'll be shot of you by the end of the month. My niece and nephew want me, if *you* don't. They've bought a little shop, see? With a flat over it, where I can live in a bit of peace, and keep an eye on things at nights with the dog here. We've been planning this for the last two months – so you don't frighten me with your high and mighty air, and your policemen. I'm glad to see the back of you.'

The venom with which this was said made Peter wonder if his neighbour were mentally unhinged. It certainly gave him some idea of the wicked malice of the woman.

'I'm glad to hear you are going. It's the best way for all of us. The sooner you can go the better, Mrs Fowler. Meanwhile, I expect you to return the sergeant's property today. If there's any hanky-panky, I fully intend to inform the police, and they can make further inquiries.'

He made his way towards the door, feeling that, although he may have had the last word, Mrs Fowler had come out of the conflict with considerable success.

But any slight chagrin was overwhelmed by the flood of relief which this news brought. She was going! The cottage would be empty!

Tyler's Row, at long last, would be all their own.

20. Double Victory

The school holidays, as always, sped past at twice the speed of term time, and it was with horrible shock that I realized that only one week remained of freedom.

Two applicants only had appeared for the advertised post of infants' teacher, and both had failed to get the job. I was beginning to brace myself for tackling the whole school single-handed next term when the vicar called.

'Good news!' were his first words. 'I've just been to see Mrs Annett, who has agreed to come for the whole of next term, unless we can get someone. Isn't that splendid?'

I agreed wholeheartedly.

Mrs Annett taught at Fairacre School before her marriage to a neighbouring headmaster. She was a first-class infants' teacher, knew the families, and we had always got on well together.

'Such a pity we could not make an appointment,' went on the vicar, looking distressed. 'But they were both *hopelessly unsuitable*. One was not a Christian, in fact, she *boasted*, there is no other word for it, about being an atheist! "Why apply for a post in a church school?" I had asked her. And she had the impertinence to say that even atheists had to live.'

'What about the other one?'

'A most admirable character, but she had an invalid husband, a mother of ninety-two living with her, and six children, some quite young. We were much touched by her case, but in fairness to the children at Fairacre School, and to you too, Miss Read, we felt we could not possibly appoint someone with so many commitments already. We feared that there were bound to be periods when she could not get to school. A sad case, a very sad case. I made it my business to get in touch with her parish priest – a new fellow evidently. I think he may be able to help.'

I had no doubt that our good Mr Partridge had already sent help via the said parish priest. His stipend is small, for the living of Fairacre is not a rich one, but those in need never go away from the vicarage empty-handed. The poor woman may not have secured the post, but she had made a staunch friend in our vicar, and some lightening of her burden would assuredly be forthcoming.

'I wondered whether to call on Miss Clare yet again,' went on the vicar, 'but she is really so frail, particularly since dear Emily's death, that it seemed hardly fair to suggest it. But Mrs Annett was a brainwave of my own!'

He looked as pleased as a child who has put the last piece into an intricate jigsaw puzzle. I congratulated him warmly.

'Well, there it is,' he said happily, collecting his things together. 'That's all settled. Mrs Annett can be here for a whole term, if need be.'

'But only for a term,' I pointed out. 'We must still advertise for a permanent teacher.'

His face puckered with dismay. 'Yes, yes. Of course we must. I suppose we *shall* get someone?'

'We'll live in hope,' I said firmly, leading him to the gate.

That evening Amy called to deliver some plants.

'I promised you these,' she told me, depositing several large, damp newspaper parcels on my nicely scrubbed kitchen table.

'What are they?'

Amy swiftly poured out a torrent of dog Latin which meant nothing to me, and I said so.

'What sort of flowers do they have?'

'Fairly insignificant. It's the *foliage* which is the chief attraction.'

'No real flowers?' I cried in dismay. 'I like nice bright things like nasturtiums and marigolds.'

'So anyone can see from your primitive flower garden,' said

Amy. 'You really haven't progressed from the mustard-and-cress stage of horticulture.'

'Well, thank you anyway,' I said nobly, remembering my manners. 'I'll put them in before I go to bed.'

'James and I are going off for a week in Scotland,' Amy said, lighting a cigarette from an exquisite gold lighter. 'Vanessa's up there already, incidentally. A friend of her mother's runs a hotel near Aberdeen, and she's gone up to help. I must say, she's a changed girl. I tell Gerard it was largely his doing.'

'How's the Bolivian heart-throb?'

'In prison, I hope. Thank God that phase is over. In fact, she's met a Scotch – or is it Scots or Scottish? – boy, who is being very attentive. He's very handsome, according to Vanessa, and wears the kilt. Now, why *the* kilt? It sounds as though the whole male population only owns one garment between the lot of them, doesn't it?'

'Do you think she might be serious?'

'Well, she's sent a photograph of him, and he has quite beautiful knees above those long woolly socks with tags sticking out at the top. And he's six-foot-three, and sturdily built. "Braw", I suppose, is the word. I must say he's a very personable young man, and has some money too, which always helps.'

'I hope something comes of it. She looked ripe for matrimony, to my eye.'

Amy looked at me speculatively. 'You don't feel drawn that way yourself?'

'No, Amy dear, I don't. I'm really too busy to get married, even if anyone wanted me.'

'It was a pity about Gerard –' began Amy.

'No, it wasn't,' I broke in. 'Gerard Baker no more wants to marry than I do. If only people like you would face the fact that there are marrying folk and non-marrying folk, the world would be a much simpler place.'

'I suppose so,' admitted Amy. She blew a smoke ring, and

watched it float through the French window and across the despised marigolds outside.

'He has a rather interesting bachelor friend –' she began dreamily.

'*Amy!*' I shouted. 'You are absolutely incorrigible! Have some coffee?'

'An excellent idea!' said Amy, swiftly abandoning her matchmaking.

Mr Willet came up to the school to mend the refractory skylight.

'Love's labour lost,' he commented, gazing up at it. 'It's the one job in this 'ere village as gives no satisfaction. Gardening, cuttin' hedges, diggin' a grave, paintin' the house – they all gives you some reward, but this 'ere skylight leaks again as soon as it's done. Still, 'ere goes!'

He began to climb the ladder, but paused on the third rung.

'Heard the news from Tyler's Row? That Mrs Fowler's leavin'. Goin' to live with her niece and nephew at Caxley, she says. Makes out it was all arranged afore the fuss about old Burnaby's things, but I bet that's all my eye and Betty Martin.'

'So both cottages are empty then?'

'That's right. Sergeant Burnaby's bits and pieces went over to Beech Green the day before yesterday. He'll be a sight better off with the Bennetts than scratchin' along on his own, poor old fellow, and I bet the Hales will be glad to get the place to theirselves at last. They done wonders with the middle bit, my wife says. Be a treat to see that place pulled up together. It's years since anyone took an interest in it.'

'Maybe it will become a shrine for Loyshus when Mr Baker's book comes out.'

'Been plenty of other funny souls dwellin' under that roof,' commented Mr Willet. 'Remember Sally Gray, as took to flyin'? I told you about her one day. Got a nice headstone, Sally has, in the churchyard. Don't make 'em like that any more.' He climbed up two rungs and looked towards the village. 'Here comes that Mrs Johnson. I'll get started.'

He scampered up the ladder with the agility of a ten-year-old, and left me to face my visitor alone.

'I come on a sad errand,' began Mrs Johnson, looking anything but sad I thought.

'Not the children? They are well, I hope?'

'Perfectly, thank you, and out on their Holiday Project at the moment.'

'What's that?'

' "The Conditions of the Rural Poor. Are we still Two Nations?" It involves a certain amount of calling at the cottages, of course, and asking people about their incomes, and how they manage their housekeeping, and so on.'

I was staggered. The thought of the three Johnson children laying themselves open to lashing tongues and well-aimed cuffs appalled me.

'People have been so cooperative,' went on Mrs Johnson. 'It's amazing how wages differ, and some of the men spend over five pounds on beer, and their wives often buy steak and oysters.'

This was so patently outrageous that I saw that Fairacre was positively enjoying its leg-pulling. Trust a countryman to have the last laugh.

The wind began to blow fragments of old paint and splinters of wood from Mr Willet's handiwork.

'Come inside,' I said, 'out of the mess.'

The school had its chilly holiday stillness about it, the smell of Mrs Pringle's yellow soap and black-lead. The nature table, the cupboard tops, the window sills were all uncannily bare. The whole place seemed derelict despite its tidiness. For one moment – a very brief one – I longed for the beginning of term, for voices and laughter and the school bell ringing high above.

'The fact is, Miss Read,' said Mrs Johnson, seating herself on a desk lid, 'we are moving back to London. It's promotion for my husband, and frankly we shall all be glad to get back to civilization. It's been an interesting interlude in our lives – I don't think any of us quite realized how *primitive* conditions still were in some parts of this country, but we shall be glad to get back to some *intelligent* and *cultured* society.'

'Of course,' I said politely.

'I do regret having to give up my part in the Parent–Teacher Association, but it's nice to know that the good work will go on.'

'I suppose so,' I replied, trying not to sound regretful.

'Mrs Mawne has been briefed, and I think the autumn programmes I have sketched out will carry you through until you can manage for yourselves.'

At this moment, I was spared replying by the advent of Mrs Pringle, who entered carrying an interesting-looking parcel wrapped in a snowy teacloth.

'Brought you a fowl. It's one of my brother's, and I've got it ready for the table, knowing you. I'd be ashamed to admit I couldn't draw a bird and dress it for the table, but there it is – If you can't, you can't.'

I thanked her sincerely, and said I would go and get my purse.

'I would've left it in the porch but for that cat of yourn. I didn't know you was busy.'

She cast a dour glance upon Mrs Johnson. 'Those desks', she said heavily, 'have been polished.'

Mrs Johnson rose hastily, and followed me to the door. Mrs Pringle brought up the rear.

I was about to go across to the house when Mr Willet called me. The next few minutes were spent in shouting to each other about the state of the skylight, but I could hear Mrs Johnson's and Mrs Pringle's conversation much more clearly than our own.

'I must say,' said Mrs Johnson, after explaining that her family were moving, 'it will be a relief to get the children into proper schools again. With the help we've been able to give them at home, they have *just* kept their heads above water in this backward place. But it's certainly been a great struggle.'

Mrs Pringle's face was as red as a turkey-cock's. She seemed to have swollen to twice her size. I began to tremble for Mrs Johnson's safety.

'Let me tell you,' boomed Mrs Pringle, prodding Mrs Johnson's chest with a fore-finger like a pork sausage, 'that you won't find a better school than this one in the length and breadth of the land! Nor a better teacher'n our Miss Read. I've seen plenty of teachers come and go over the years, and though she may not be *Tidy*, she can learn them children better'n any of 'em. I won't hear a word against her.'

I clung to Mr Willet's ladder with shock.

Feeling the tremor he looked down at me anxiously. 'You all right? You gone a bit pale.'

'I'm fine,' I croaked. And I felt it.

Mrs Johnson set off in silence, away from her adversary, and I found my voice in time to shout after her. 'Goodbye, Mrs Johnson. Good luck!'

She acknowledged my farewells with a stiff nod, and vanished round the corner of the lane.

Mrs Pringle, still bearing the snowy parcel, accompanied me across the playground to the school house.

'Cheek!' she muttered under her breath, still smouldering. 'The sauce! The upstart! Good riddance to bad rubbish! London, indeed! It's welcome to her!'

I fetched my purse and put money into her hand. Her face was still rosy with wrath.

'Thank you, Mrs Pringle,' I said. 'Thank you for everything.'

Mrs Fowler moved out of Tyler's Row three days before Peter returned to school. The shabby van made several trips back and forth to Caxley. Sergeant Burnaby's treasures had been returned, and were now with their rightful owner at Beech Green.

Mrs Fowler left the cottage spotlessly clean. Nothing which she had bought was left in place. Even the electric light blubs had been taken.

Diana was the last person to see her. Mrs Fowler brought the key, and was about to slip it through the letter box and depart, but Diana, who felt that she could not let the old lady go in such a mood, opened the door and spoke to her.

'Goodbye, Mrs Fowler. I hope you'll be happy in Caxley.'

'A fat lot happier than I've been here,' replied Mrs Fowler viciously. 'I'm glad to see the back of Tyler's Row.'

She thrust the key at Diana, and stalked away to the waiting van, her back as straight as a ramrod, registering malice to the last.

'She enjoys it, my dear,' Peter said when Diana told him

later. 'What you won't understand is that some people thoroughly enjoy a fight. They're hawks by nature. You're a dove, and a particularly soft-hearted one. Rather a rare bird, in fact.' He smiled affectionately at his wife. 'Shall we go out and celebrate our freedom?'

'No, I'd sooner stay here and enjoy the wonderful feeling of peace,' said Diana. 'I can't really believe that at last Tyler's Row is our own.'

'Not for long,' Peter warned her. 'Soon it will all begin again – the bricklayers, the plumbers, the electricians, the painters, the plasterers. Cups of coffee for old Fairbrother and those transistor-mad maniacs of his. Chaos all over again!'

'I can face it,' said Diana. 'I can face anything at the moment.'

Later that evening she went into the garden to pick some mint. Darkness was falling, and a light mist veiled the downs. Early Michaelmas daisies starred the border, and the last few yellow roses on Sergeant Burnaby's wall were dropping their petals. Autumn was in the air. Soon it would be time to light bonfires, to stack logs and to prepare for their first winter at Tyler's Row.

Holding the cool stalks of the mint, she looked at their home. There it stood, as it had done for generations, silvery thatched, ancient and snug, melting into the shadowy background of trees and downland. How many men and women who had lived there, thought Diana, had stood as she did now, looking upon their home, and finding it good?

The windows glowed from the dark bulk of the building. Diana, shivering with the first chill touch of autumn, went thankfully towards the warm haven of Tyler's Row.

Peter was telephoning when she opened the door. There was a look of utter contentment on his face.

'Any time you like, Bellamy,' he was saying. 'Any time you like.'

He held out his free hand to Diana, and they stood there, hand in hand like two children. His voice became triumphant. 'Stage Two can begin!'